Erich Romberg

Mystical stories in and about Ireland

About the stories in the stories

Vol. 2

Dedication

The Art

Storytelling is an intimate and interactive art. A storyteller tells from memory rather than reading from a book. A tale is not just the spoken equivalent of a literary short story. It has no set text, but is endlessly re-created in the telling. The listener is an essential part of the storytelling process. For stories to live, they need the hearts, minds and ears of listeners. Without the listener there is no story.

www.storytellersofireland.org

Erich Romberg

Mystical stories in and about Ireland

About the stories in the stories

Vol. 2

Dangerous encounter on the One Man's Pass

Imprint

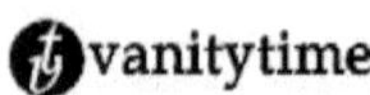 vanitytime

© 2024 Erich Romberg

Cover artwork by: Freepik

 Printing and distribution by order of the author:

tredition GmbH, Heinz-Beusen-Stieg 5, 22926 Ahrensburg, Germany

ISBN
Paperback   978-3-384-12824-9
Hardcover   978-3-384-12825-6
E-Book   978-3-384-12826-3

Email: storyteller@vanitytime.de

Table of Contents

Foreword

In the foreword to the first volume, the author goes into detail about his motivation for publishing the series of stories. In the following volumes, he confines himself to the content of the respective volume.

As in the first volume, the author gives voice to fictional narrators in this second volume. The only thing that is real is the way in which the stories are told, as experienced by the author, and to some extent the background to the stories told. The author leaves it up to the attentive reader to judge which stories could have a real background. But be careful, it is easy to be deceived.

In the first story, the narrator finds himself on death row. He is said to be a parricide.

In the title story, the narrator ventures up the legendary One Man's Pass on the cliffs of Slieve League one day despite his fear of heights. At a particularly narrow point, of all places, where no two people can pass each other, he has a dangerous encounter with a stranger who moves safely up here.

Nobody wants to back down, but does he have a choice? Then the stranger makes a surprising proposal.

In the third story, the narrator picks up an old hitchhiker in Kinnegad late at night in stormy weather and is drawn by her into a maelstrom of eerie stories dating back to the sixteenth century. Has he fallen into the night of the eternal judgement of blood, a curse from the past? On this night, the devil takes a traveller every 70 years at the hands of an old woman who joins him on the road.

The author then gives the floor to a storyteller from Donegal. He tells four stories:

How do you become a dream designer? The first story provides the answer. The author has borrowed a little from Novalis here.

In the second story, he tells of a man who must have realised for a moment that his vanity was nothing.

The third story is about a ruler whose greed for power and vanity lead to his downfall.

The last story is about addiction, deception and self-deception.

The author really lets it rip in the last story. It is guaranteed to have no deeper meaning. As Albert Einstein so aptly put it:

Even the senseless still has a loose meaning.

About love (poetry)

Soul, your fairest brightest gift,
Orpheus this once sang about,
is your most sacred desire,
is the womb that unites us.

Joy that is your holy lyre,
lets your loveliest song ring out,
Love is called your precious giftedness,
Out of chaos, she gave us life.

Soul, your fairest brightest gift,
Entity of earliest time,
just like Gaya, our mother,
Seed you have prepared to sow.

Soul, in blooming summer time,
you weave us a golden dress,
let us fall in loving arms,

dwelling there for all our time.

Time and vanity (poetry calligramm)

Fleeing his transience, human being creates foolish things at the fairground of life.
He wants to erect unmistakable monuments, proof of being, of having been.
Like a drowning man, he clings to the skeleton of his individuality.
Extroverted, he makes his mark in order to be recognised.
But time is the incorruptible enforcer of the vanity.
Years and millennia pass all over everyone,
over man and his sad individuality;
over all that he has ever been,
he had thought or created.
Even the greatest of us
is devoured by the
wild predator
time.

A memorable dream

On a warm weekend night in summer, when the hustle and bustle of the disco at the Cill Aodain Court Hotel had died down, I sat with a few friends in Joyce's. Paul locked the door and drew the curtains in front of the windows. The lights were dimmed and a peat fire lit. Joyce's didn't have a night licence. First they had a drink. Then Paul asked if anyone wanted to tell a story. I said that someone had told me a dream years ago, which, as usual, he had not forgotten and would never forget.

I asked the group what they thought about the fourth commandment from the second book of Moses. Very spontaneously, everyone pretty much agreed that it should be obeyed exactly as it is written in the Bible. I followed up:

"So you should put your parents on a pedestal, no matter what they did to you?"

"What do parents do to a child?" asked anybody of the group, "a slap behind the ears? That never hurt anyone."

How did he know that it wouldn't have harmed anyone, are there any studies?

There's no need for studies, everyone has had a spanking or two as a child and they are all healthy and coping with life.

I asked if anyone had ever heard of Munchausen's proxy syndrome.
Parents deliberately hurt their children and then take care of them in public.

Nobody would do such a thing, they were sure.

But, I said, the English paediatrician Roy Meadow was the first to write about such cases from his practice in 'The Lancet' in 1977. Thousands of cases are now known. Then I said:

"Well, I didn't really want to talk about that, people who are more familiar with it will do that. I just needed a transition to my next story. I'll tell it as if I'd had the dream myself. I can't guarantee that it was told in exactly the same way, but the essentials are included. Just imagine that the protagonist of the dream experienced what I have described above. Or he has other valid reasons why he cannot honour his father and mother, as required by the fourth commandment. No third party is allowed to judge this; only the person concerned can judge. I am sending this in advance so that you do not judge my protagonist too quickly. After all, he didn't murder his parents, he dreamt that he had done it. I have the impression that the dreamer's subconscious has triggered something that he had repressed for a long time. A tin whistle is strangely interwoven in this dream. That's why I called this story 'The Whistle':"

The Whistle

I can't even play her properly. Don't get me wrong, I can play her, but not the way I want to.

My whistle is handmade, a genuine Overton tin whistle. I own many tin whistles, English ones made of steel, Irish ones made of brass, in C major, in D major, in every key. They sound tinny and shrill, but none of them is like her.

When I hold my whistle in my hands, she feels soft and warm. She is made of matt aluminium and has the six holes of a tin whistle, but she is something special. The way she feels is the way she sounds. Not that you think she's easy to play. I mean, it's as easy to play as a tin whistle- technically, but she's not easy to speak to her soul. My tin whistle has a soul. So you have to play she with soul to ignite her warmth and fire. Used without feeling, she blocks. She simply stops making sounds. Then I knock her out because she is clogged with saliva. Then she plays for a while, but then she refuses again. She can be very stubborn, but on those days, when she feels soft and warm, she is willing, then she makes me believe that I am playing her, but she is playing me. I close my eyes and hold her in my hands, soft and warm. A melody resonates in me that she projects, a warmth that she radiates, a fire that fills the room. In these moments we are one, not whistle and flutist, but just me.

***

Now I'm sitting here, on death row - without her. I wasn't given the time to look for her. Yes, you can believe me, I should have looked for her at the crucial moment. Forgetting her was normal for me, how often had I misplaced her. At times I didn't even think about her, I lived my life without her. But from time to time, often in difficult times, I missed her. I became restless and obnoxious. I just wanted to find my whistle. Like a man possessed, I searched for her, turned flats upside down and accused friends of stealing her. In those moments, I realised that I couldn't live without her. I found her again and again, she spoilt me with her most beautiful sounds, she felt soft and warm. She never took offence at my neglect. How often was she especially loving towards me after a long period of carelessness.

At those times, her sounds resonated with the

vibrations of my soul.

I'm sitting here waiting to die. I think I killed my father, or my mother. Maybe I killed them both, I don't know for sure. They told me I was a parricide and that's why I had to die. I realised that, because in this country parricides have to die. But they taught me that you don't kill parents. I did it anyway. They taught me that you have to honour and love your father and mother, but I killed them anyway. Now I sit here and wait for my just punishment. Yesterday, my brother and sister visited me. I asked them to bring me my whistle, but they said that I am evil because I killed my father and mother.

They loved me very much, but I didn't thank them.

That's why I deserve to die. I realised that. They didn't want to look for my whistle.

That was yesterday, and they said they wouldn't come back - until then.

I sit here alone, waiting to die, missing my whistle. I hear footsteps that I know are coming to me.

It's my carer. He looks at me with compassion.

"You will be executed on Monday. The request for a pardon has been rejected."

I look this poor man in the eye, he is visibly affected.

"It's only a small step," I try to comfort him.

"I know," he says, "but it would be so easy to change that. I've realised for so long that nobody needs to be executed, but there's nothing I can do about it."

I look at my warder. He's sitting huddled on my cot, a heap of misery. I feel very sorry for him, this poor man.

Suddenly the colour of his face changes, he seems determined, but his eyes still show hopelessness.

"Let me do something for you - please."

I don't have to think:

"I need my whistle, an aluminium tin whistle. I couldn't find her when they came to pick me up."

At this moment, the guard's face brightens.

"Is she an Overton that sometimes feels soft and warm?"

He looks at me hopefully. I don't have to explain anything to him, he is also a whistle player.

"I'll find her!" he says.

There are still three nights until Monday, but I'm

not worried. My warder will find her.

Another guard arrives on Saturday - he's not a whistle player. He tells me that his colleague is looking for something important, but he doesn't know what.

On Sunday evening, I hear those footsteps again, which I know are coming to me. With a beaming face, my warder hands me the whistle.

"Everything will be fine now," he says. I take her and say: "Yes!"

He looks at me and admonishes me:

"But don't play until tomorrow when they've picked you up. I'll be with you."

I look at him lovingly and reassure him:

"You can go now, it's all done."

The next morning, I hear many footsteps that I also know are coming towards me. I clutch my whistle tightly.

The cell door flies open and grim faces look at me. An important-looking man dressed in black reads to me from an important-looking document that I have killed my father or my mother, or both. In any case, I would be hung by the neck until death. They lead me through a long dark corridor. An indeterminate number of people walk in front of me and another indeterminate number walk behind me. We enter a high room with a platform in the centre. A gallows with a noose made of thick rope dangling about fifty centimetres above the floor of the platform protrudes from it. I know this is the noose that will be placed around my neck.

There are a lot of people in the execution room, they all want to see a parricide die. I can see my brother and sister in the front row. Sitting near them are nephews, nieces, uncles and aunts. They are all waiting for the brother, uncle or nephew to be executed for killing their parents, aunt, uncle, brother or sister. They all know that I deserve this punishment.

As I stand at the top of the platform, this important-looking official reads from the important-looking document that I have killed my father, or mother, or both, and will therefore be hanged by the neck until death occurs. I see my brother and sister applauding in the first row of spectators. My eyes search for my keeper, but they can't find him. The whole time I clutch my whistle tightly with my right hand, but the absence of my keeper worries me. The important-looking official has just finished reading from that very document. He looks at me and asks if I have any other requests.

At that moment, someone taps me on the shoulder. I look around and recognise my guard, he is the executioner. He looks me kindly in the eye and says:

"Ask them to play one last piece on your whistle."

I am allowed to do so and my warder puts the noose round my neck.

"Have faith in me and in your whistle," he says.

I take her in both hands and she feels soft and warm.

Undeterred, she plays 'Once Upon a Time in the West', the melody of which I could never remember.

"Trust your whistle," my executioner repeats and pulls the lever to the trapdoor.

The flap opens and the melody of death drifts lonesomely on the wind.

***

"Then my protagonist woke up and the melody ' Once Upon a Time in the West ' was still ringing in his ears."

The redeemed self (poetry)

Worldliness slips away from the ego,
it flows without restraint.
The meagre nourishment is consumed.
It clings desperately to the now.

Maya is essence-free,
transformation to the point of dissipation.
Redemption is promised by a reflection on the
horizon,
a luminescent myth.

Projection from infinity.
Being strives longingly towards the absolute,
creating in order
to escape its dissolution.

Eating one's fill of the unattainable goal,
a piece of eternity.
Dilating towards one's own creator,
creating from the ashes.

Rising like a phoenix.
The myth beckons from infinity.
The premonition of the absolute
speaks from his creations.

But the horizon does not light itself;
thinking does not end at the horizon,
crossing it
is a first step towards infinity.

This step is the work
and every step is a new horizon.
The creator gazes into infinity,
gazing without accommodation.

Search with earthly works,
manifested in the earthly.
Allegorised eternity
in order to escape ego dissipation.

The creator strives towards the absolute,
towards ego expansion,
step by step,
from horizon to horizon.

The ego longs for redemption,
from the earthly, from death.
It wants to become a part,
a part of the eternal myth.

The secret of life (poetry)

Life is a sphere
on whose surface we live.
We have every freedom to move around
on this surface.
Sometimes we cross points that
we have already touched,
déjà vu.
But we know nothing of the depth of this sphere,
it lies beyond our imagination.
We do not realise
that the centre is not in our lives,
but in this depth.

On the Cliffs of the Slieve Leagues

At a cosy peat fire on a weekend night in Kiltimagh, I rejoined the hard core of remainers. For some reason we got talking about Slieve League and its One Man's Pass, which none of us had ever walked. Adventurous stories were told that were only hearsay.

"I've been toying with the idea of doing One Man's Pass for a long time," I said to the group. "Until now, I only knew that this strange pass involves a huge up and down to the summit of Slieve League."

In fact, One Man's Pass is part of a larger network of more or less challenging paths that lead over the steep cliffs of the Slieve Leagues. This cliff in Donegal is one of the highest in Europe. In many places a person can barely get around, so it's better not to risk oncoming traffic with people returning from the 601-metre summit as you climb it. I'm not a big fan of high, steep heights with unsafe paths, which is one of the reasons why I've never climbed all the way to the top. Also, respect for the name, which states that the width of the path only allows one person to walk it, made me turn back again and again. I never actually walked it and made do with the less risky paths of the Slieve Leagues for my hikes, which offer wonderful viewpoints even without this risk. Now such walks are beautiful, but not very spectacular to talk about. That's why, in the following story, I walk this path together with my listeners and readers.

 I already had the story written in my bag, so I didn't have to tell it off the cuff. I told the story from my manuscript:

One Man's Pass

Dangerous encounter on the One Man's Pass

I have always tried to overcome my awe of this path. From One Man's Pass, there are many places with a drop of more than five hundred metres. A strong wind often blows up there and on the west side, the Atlantic crashes against the coast. Once I was able to observe how shreds of the surf were sucked up to this path. There are certainly days when I would have lacked the courage. But on this day, the weather seemed favourable for such an undertaking. There was only a gentle breeze here in the village and it wasn't going to be too stormy on the west coast of Donegal that day either. It was also midweek and outside of the holidays, so an unpleasant encounter in unfavourable places was unlikely.

It took me a good two hours to get to Teelin and I drove straight up the switchbacks to Bunglass Point and from there up to Amharic Mor at Slieve Leagues, where I had often parked my car. From here it's a walk only, and I had to climb for about twenty-five minutes to reach the strange path. Now I stood in front of the short steep slope that I still had to overcome and set foot on it for the first time.

The wind up here was between three and four,

the weather was stable, so I didn't expect any difficulties. It was only because of the strong wind that I had often not taken the risk.

The actual One Man's Pass is about three kilometres long and it was clear to me that the initially gentle gradient of the path would not stay that way. The path narrowed almost imperceptibly at first and it was only when it was only sixty to seventy centimetres wide that I realised how steeply the terrain fell away on both sides of the path. From that moment on, I felt my weight, barely daring to look to the side. I stared, mesmerised, at the narrow path that seemed to be the only one up here. When the path became even narrower, I didn't dare go any further. The force of the depths pulled me. The path began to sway, I couldn't stand it any longer and sat down. What demon must have been riding me when I embarked on this foolish adventure. Sitting down, I felt safe again and dared to look around. I was startled, infinity was grinning at me. I had been so lost in thought on the way here that I hadn't even realised the distance I had travelled.

"I have to get used to it first," I said to myself quietly, but it didn't convince me. I thought about the psychological causes of my condition, but what good did that do at that moment, I didn't dare get up and keep walking. I closed my eyes and felt the wind picking up. I couldn't sit like this forever. I must have lost my sense of time, because I didn't know whether the way forwards or backwards was the shorter one.

I cautiously opened my eyes again and dared to look down at the land to orientate myself. I couldn't recognise anything, just the immense depth. I now also looked at the sea and realised that my situation wasn't that bad, "I must get used to it," I said to myself again, and this time it convinced me. Determined, I got up and continued on my way. I didn't dare look to the side, trying to suppress the rising panic, but my legs became soft and trembling. I risked a careless glance downwards and it pulled me off my feet. It was only with difficulty that I managed to escape the downward pull. I clung to the rocky ground on my knees, the abyss wanted to swallow me up. I remembered the parable of the fallen rider, who can only ride on if he does so immediately.

Trembling, I stood up; I knew that nothing else made sense. Never before had I realised how difficult it would be to escape the compulsion to look into the depths. I knew I wasn't allowed to, and yet I couldn't look away. The path began to sway again and my legs threatened to give out. Then came the unexpected rescue, the path opened up more and more and was now almost twice as wide. Relieved, I stopped and took a deep breath. What sensitive beings we humans are. Now my behaviour seemed exaggerated and I laughed out loud. The chasms on either side no longer seemed threatening. I continued on my way with courageous steps.

"I can do it," I said to myself and felt as if I had just defeated a dangerous monster. But suddenly the path became narrower and steeper again and I felt my old fears returning. Had I been arrogant three hundred metres earlier? I mustered all my strength and managed to keep my eyes away from the abyss, but my thoughts saw it too. I stretched my arms out to both sides, like a tightrope walker, so as not to lose my balance. I moved forwards, always afraid of taking a wrong step. Worried, I noticed that the wind was getting stronger and stronger. The sky was closing in at breakneck speed and I could feel disaster looming. I didn't know how long I had been travelling or how much further it would be. I had lost all sense of direction. I remembered that I only knew the length of One Man's Pass from stories, or was it miles? I regretted that I hadn't checked. This was the first time it occurred to me that it would be better to turn back. I knew the narrow sections in this direction; I would certainly master them again. But I only knew what lay ahead of me from stories told by people who hadn't walked it themselves. What I knew from the stories didn't exactly make me confident. What's more, I would definitely have to return the way I had come, as there is only the "One Man's Pass" back from the summit.

Then I saw the unbelievable thing I hadn't thought of. Something appeared on the horizon and came towards me on the path. It couldn't be, it couldn't be..., I didn't want to believe it, my God, now it was clear: someone was coming towards me with quick steps. I was overcome with fear, I had suppressed this possibility, I had completely repressed it. Here, in this narrow place, we would come face to face. I no longer dared to go any further. Besides, I couldn't see a wider space between me and the stranger walking towards me. From the level of the cliff crest on which you walk here, there is a steep drop on both sides, everywhere.

My mind was racing: how were we going to get

past each other? There's only room for one; turning back is out of the question; the last wide section is a long way behind me. Would the stranger retreat? What was he doing here? My legs threatened to give out again and I sat down. I couldn't show any fear. But I knew I wouldn't be able to hold my own against him; surely he was marching over the ridge. I turned my gaze to the sea as if I was enjoying the view. There wasn't enough room behind me to let the stranger pass.

Then he stood there. There was a broad, unpleasant grin on his face. I noticed that he was very tall. His face showed no fear and he made no effort to sit down.

"Nice view," he said.

"Yes," I said, endeavouring not to let my voice tremble.

"Not many people take this route, but I like it. It has character, especially in this weather." He looked around with pleasure.

"Yes, that's right," I said, thinking that he must realise I was lying.

"I've never seen you up here before." The stranger looked at me expectantly.

"I'm here for the first time too, how far is it to the summit?"

"I've never counted the steps," said the stranger, "but there are still a lot of them and it's getting steeper and steeper. You have to climb the last bit. But the view is great and it keeps pulling you up."

I couldn't really understand his soft spot at that moment. He turned towards the coast and gazed into the distance, lost in thought. After a while, he looked at me and said:

"If we both turn our backs to the abyss, we'll pass each other and you won't have to turn round until we reach the widest part. There are no wider places further up for a long time."

The possibility of turning back himself was obviously an option for him. Besides, he would always be behind me if I turned back. Fear crept up my spine, the thought of slipping past him, death right behind me, was not encouraging. I looked into his grinning face, wasn't there malice in his eyes? I would be completely at his mercy and I wouldn't stand a chance against malice. I saw no other way out and tried a little honesty:

"I don't think I'm up to it, you have to remember

that it's my first time up here and I still have to get used to this altitude."

The stranger frowned.

"That's what I thought, but we have to find a solution. We both still have a long way to go."

After one look at his enormous stature, I knew that whatever he suggested, I had to accept it. He looked at the sea again and said nothing for a long time. An arm's length away from me, he stood close to the edge, so close that his toes stuck out over the edge. He looked down steeply. He seemed immune to the pull of the depths. How easy it would have been for me to give him a push here to clear the way. But I was immediately ashamed that I had even allowed this thought to occur to me. But the devil inside me whispered, what if he was thinking the same thing at that moment? If he had made up his mind, it would be too late. I would never get that chance again. I didn't have the courage to hit him, but maybe I had simply overcome the devil in me. I was surprised that I was even capable of such thoughts. Now he squatted next to me, then he said:

"It doesn't make much sense to go back the way I came, because there are no more plateaus to

avoid, or only very late, and then we would almost be at the top. We obtain a judgement from God, whoever loses must turn back."
 What did he mean? If I lost, I would have him at my back the whole way, at least until we reached the wide part of the path.

"What do you mean?"
"Do you know the puzzle
 decisions?"

I know that from The Hobbit, for example, when he was puzzling with Gollum. As far as I remember, it was also a matter of life and death. I used to play it with fellow students when I was younger; one would set a puzzle and the other would have to solve it. Whoever lost had to pay for the next round of beer. Of course, that's only a small prize, so you didn't have to be particularly ambitious.

But here it means that we set each other riddles. If you don't solve the puzzle, you have to bend to the will of the other person. But at least I have an honest chance,

"Yes," I said, trying to take the initiative, "let's toss a coin to see who gets to pose the first riddle".

The stranger grinned broadly and said,

"Agreed."

He pulled a fifty pence coin out of his pocket and let me vote. The decision went against me.

"The puzzle decision must be accepted," said the stranger, "unfairness is out of the question." 'Who will judge it afterwards,' I thought. As if he had guessed my thoughts, he said:

"God is our witness."

That's good, if the stranger is Irish - and I assumed he was - then he'll stick to the rules. An Irishman would never call God to witness if he intended to cheat.

"God will be our witness," I said.

"Then we can be sure that we're both being fair," he began: "Listen carefully, here's my first riddle: give me a plausible example of what eternity means."

My heart leapt for joy because I knew the answer. Without thinking, I shot off.

"Eternity is indescribable and timeless, it cannot be grasped by us humans. But there is a story that gives us a glimpse of the secret. I don't know exactly what this story is or who told it. Let's assume: A long time ago, a Zen student asked his master this question. The master answered it:

In a distant world, there is a diamond mountain. It has a height that a full-grown man can cover in a day if he walks fast. It takes him the same amount of time to walk up to the other side of the mountain and the same amount of time to walk down. Every thousand years a small bird flies up this mountain and sharpens its beak once. After the time when this mountain is completely worn down, the first second of eternity has not yet passed.

 The stranger was silent for a moment, then he looked at me and said:

"I can't give you a better description than that. I think I heard a similar story in a fairy tale. But that's irrelevant, you've solved the riddle, now tell me yours."

I had to think for a moment, then I had an idea: "Who is your constant companion? He asks no questions and gives no answers. He's sometimes big, sometimes small, hides in the dark and follows your every move."

The wind swept sharply up the slope. The stranger's eyes were fixed on the Atlantic, his hair flying wildly around his head. He didn't waver an inch in the increasingly violent, hissing gusts. Since I had just invented the riddle, he couldn't have the answer ready. Time passed and hope grew that he wouldn't come up with it. I waited patiently. A quarter of an hour might have passed when he turned to me again:

"It's the shadow?"

He had figured it out. I had to think of something more difficult next time if I wanted to get down here unscathed. But first I had to solve his riddle, which he started to do immediately.

"Where is the place where you return when you take one step southwards, one step westwards and one step northwards?"

That was easy, and if his riddles weren't any more difficult, I should be able to defeat the stranger. I got cocky and answered in a counter-mystery:
"It's the place opposite the one from which you go one step north, one step east and one step south to get back there."

Without hesitation he said:

"You solved the riddle and answered it cleverly, I like that."

His face was relaxed and he was smiling, he seemed to be enjoying himself.

"Now tell me your second riddle," he added.

I liked the situation far less than the stranger, as I believed my life was at stake. But did I still believe it? Because his words were friendly, he didn't sound sneaky. I took my time, because he didn't seem to be in a hurry. This story was slowly beginning to amuse me too, but I was still too stubborn to admit it to myself straight away. This time I had to catch him, it was increasingly about winning, having the better puzzles. I knew how difficult it is for many people to solve logical puzzles. So I came up with one.

"There are knights and rogues," I began my riddle.
 "You should know that knights always tell the truth and, of course, don't steal. Rogues, on the other hand, always lie and stealing is their favourite pastime.

A long time ago, horses were stolen from a country estate. A short time later, three men were caught by the king's guard. It was certain that one of them had stolen the horses. It was also known that at least one was a rogue and one a knight. The names of the individuals were Aiden, Brandon and Colin. The first question the judge asked Aiden was:

'Tell me Aiden, is Brandon the thief?'
Aiden replied:
'Only if Colin is a rogue is Brandon the thief.'

Then the judge asked Brandon:
'Is Collin the thief?'
'I see', and turning to Collin he asked:
'Is Aiden the thief?'
'Yes, Judge, Aiden stole the horses'.
The judge then had the thief arrested. My question now is: who did the judge have arrested?"

The stranger looked at me, perplexed, then his gaze returned to the Atlantic without making a move. After a while, he asked me without taking his eyes off the sea: "Can you repeat the riddle again?"

'I've got him' I thought and told him the story again.

"Thank you."

Now he sat down on the narrow path and put his head in his hands. He had been sitting like that for a long time, at least half an hour. I tried not to let my burgeoning triumph show, but he was too absorbed to notice anything around him. Another half an hour might have passed and I was getting impatient, because if he didn't answer, I wasn't going to gain much.

That's why I said carefully:

"Well? We can't wait here forever."

Then he suddenly looked at me and said:

"No need, Colin was the horse thief and Brandon is the only knight."

That wasn't possible, I shouldn't have given him so much time, but maybe he was just guessing. That's why I asked:

"Can you explain why?"

"Of course, I could have guessed.

Assuming Aiden is a knight, then if Colin is a rogue, Brandon would also be a rogue and the thief. If Colin was a knight, then Brandon would either have to be a knight as well, which is not possible because not all three can be knights. Colin would therefore be a rogue. Brandon would have to be a rogue, but not the thief. Then either all three would be knights or there would be no thief, both of which contradict the premise.

So Aiden must be a villain. We must therefore reverse Aiden's statement, because he is lying, as proven above. There are two possibilities for the reversal:

If Collin is a rogue, Brandon is not a thief.

If Collin is not a villain, Brandon is the thief
and, of course, a villain.

So let's hold on.
Brandon's statement was that Colin is the thief.
If he's lying, then Colin is not the thief.
 Collin says Aiden is the thief.

If Collin is telling the truth, that contradicts
Aiden's first statement. Then Brandon would be
the thief.
 So let's take the second variant. Only if Collin
is a villain is Brandon not a thief.

This is consistent with Brandon's statement, who
accuses Collin of being the thief and therefore
also a villain.
 So there are only no contradictions if Collin is
the thief. Brandon is therefore the only knight"

If this proof is too difficult for you, you can
simply skip my counterpart's proof, I can
confirm that he is right. Those who see the proof
as a challenge are welcome to rack their brains
themselves

In any case, he had solved the puzzle perfectly
and I had probably underestimated him. Next

time I should come up with an even more
difficult puzzle, the last one was still too easy.
But it had taken him a long time and he wouldn't
be able to solve a much more complicated one in
a reasonable amount of time. But how could I
think of an even more difficult one, now, on the
spur of the moment? Despite the fierce wind up
here, my forehead was covered in sweat. Then
the stranger said:

"The last riddle was very difficult for me, so I'm
going to think of something special for you now,
so pay attention:

"Everyone desires it. One has it, the other
doesn't. Those who have it have little, enough or
a lot. It does good and much evil and yet is
neither good nor evil itself.

That's a puzzle I didn't know yet. My mind was
racing and I couldn't forget the yawning depths
on both sides. I had to solve the riddle,
otherwise I had no chance. But I didn't know if I
could formulate another riddle. I couldn't grasp
it with logic. But I had to think about his riddle
first. I found it difficult to concentrate.

Everyone wanted it, including me; one has it,
the other doesn't; that can apply to anything. The
next sentence didn't help me either. If I had

something that I liked, then it was either little, enough or a lot, there was nothing else. It did both good and bad and yet was neither bad nor good itself. That had to be the key, everything else was too vague.

It could be guns, I don't like guns, and can guns do any good? For self-defence, maybe. It doesn't feel right. I was getting more and more nervous because I couldn't think of anything. Every now and then I thought about what riddle I could pose next. Then I thought I knew: it's land, land ownership. I feverishly went through the criteria.

Everyone wants land, some have it, others don't.

If you have land, it is either little, enough or much; that is also true. It does good when it gives us food, and evil when it denies us food and lets us starve. But the land itself is neither good nor evil.

"It's the land," I said quickly, but as I said it, I was overcome with a bad feeling. The stranger jumped up and looked at me in horror:

"Land can do no wrong. The land always does the right thing. If we treat it well, it gives us food; if we treat it badly, it becomes barren and denies us food. We do evil to ourselves. The land does not."

The stranger looked at me thoughtfully and said:

"It's the money."

"Money? I hadn't even thought about that."

Again he was silent for a while, then he said:

"Money doesn't seem to play a particularly important role in your life."

His voice sounded friendly now. He held out his hand to me with a smile:

"I'm John Phillips from Teelin. The puzzles have been fun, but it's getting late, come with me and be my guest tonight, I'd love to solve a few more of your puzzles, relaxed over a tea or whisky. I also have a few that you might not know. Tomorrow I'll drive you to your car, I'm sure you're not from nearby and it'll be better to drive tomorrow during the day."

He pulled me up and with a quick turn, which I didn't really notice, he stood in front of me so that I could make my way back behind him:

"You just have to do it and not think about it for long. Now I can say it, I knew straight away that you were a newcomer to windy heights and were afraid it would be reckless not to. I opted for the puzzles because it's much more fun than just rushing past each other. Besides, it wouldn't have been a good idea to climb the path to the summit alone and inexperienced. We can do it together sometime. Hold on to my jacket in the tight places, I know the path like the back of my hand. We still have about an hour and a half to walk."

He walked confidently back the way I had come from, and he still knew a shortcut. I felt safe in his wake, the depths on either side of the narrow path had lost their power. I'm sure you can understand how much I regretted my briefly diabolical thought capers. I resolved to think up another riddle for him tonight, without danger and in a cosy atmosphere, featuring not only knights and villains but also spies who can lie, but sometimes also tell the truth. Now I want to know!

***

Aphorisms

Love is a deity

Love is a deity of the first hour that created order out of chaos.

Humour

Humour is not when you make fun of others, but when you don't take yourself too seriously.

Dialogues and monologues

Monologues are the most common form of communication. In the majority of cases, dialogues are conducted as double monologues.

Injustice

Fraud begins in the mind. The first step towards injustice is self-deception.

Advantages

For every advantage you gain for yourself, someone else suffers a disadvantage.

Life

He who has not lived does not die; he only changes his state.

Children and education

Education is the art of sparing your children from making their own mistakes.

...

Give your children the freedom to grow and the boundaries to thrive.

...

Anyone who sees their children as the icing on the cake of a successful life would do well to remain childless.

...

It's not always easy to remain consistent when your child crosses the boundaries that you enjoyed crossing yourself as a child.
But it's good to remember this in order to understand your child's enjoyment of crossing boundaries.

The mysterious Inn in Moate

In Ireland, the age of the storyteller may be over, but you still have to be prepared to be unexpectedly drawn into the maelstrom of a story. When I think back to the following story, a cold shiver still runs down my spine. This story begins as banal as any story about a return journey could begin.

The ferry to Dublin Port had been delayed by three hours. An hour and a half before midnight, I finally bumped my Volvo over the tin bridge that had been extended to connect the Inishfree with Irish soil. Still a little sleepy, I held on to the steering wheel and obediently followed the waving marshals towards the harbour exit.

On the ferry I had, thankfully, been able to sleep for three hours on a bench in Paddy Reily's pub. As I drove towards the Irish policeman at the exit of the port, I felt a little sleepy, but otherwise fit.

"A nice day," he greeted me and took my passport, which he didn't really look at.
"Yes, very nice."

A typical conversation developed, as I have had many times in this or similar ways.

"Get home safely and good luck," he finally said.

Only the weather wasn't addressed this time. But it

will play a major role in this story.
 So I was back in Ireland. I mechanically steered my Volvo, loaded with all the goods for spoilt Germans, along the Liffey towards the national roads to the west. The M50 and M4 motorways were still piecemeal, so most of the roads heading west were still routed through the villages.
 I had already left Enfield behind me and it was almost half an hour before midnight. The road was only lightly travelled and tiredness was trying to get the better of me. Nevertheless, I reached Kinnegad and turned onto the national road towards Galway. Just after the fork in the road, an old woman stood at the side of the road and pointed with her thumb in my direction. I couldn't believe my eyes - there stood an eighty-year-old hitchhiker. My tired mind awoke to this unexpected chance of a travelling companion. I stopped the vehicle in front of her and she walked towards the driver's door with incredible vigour. She was a little surprised when she saw that the seat was already occupied, but then she realised:
"It's a left-hand drive car."

Satisfied with her analysis, she moved confidently around the front of my car, confidently pulled open the passenger door and swung herself onto the seat in one leap.

"You're German? Nice people. I live in Moate."
"It's on the way."
"Fine, would you give me a lift?"
How could I not, she was already inside.
"Nice day." It was the start of the usual small talk.
I learnt that my companion's name was Maria, she
was 75 years old, she had a daughter in Castlebar
and had visited a cousin in Kinnegad.
"God bless you for taking me home."
"I'd love to, my ferry was three hours late and it's
very tiring travelling alone. I feel fitter with your
company."
"Yes, very tiring," she nodded.
"I would have liked to have a cup of tea
somewhere, but the pubs have already closed."
"You'll get your tea in Moate," Maria promised.

"Is there still a pub open there?"
"No, but we can get in."

I was looking forward to that. My companion
looked confidently ahead. We had already passed
Kilbeggan and didn't say another word.

The village of Moate seemed completely deserted
and I couldn't imagine where I would be able to get
a cup of tea.

"Are you sure we can still get in somewhere,
Maria?"

"Of course. Park the car there in the open space, can you see the pub on the right?"
 "I can't see any lights."
 "That doesn't matter."

Maria jumped out of the car with incredible agility as soon as I had stopped.

"Come, come," she ordered as I stretched my limbs, "we have to go this way."

She pointed to a narrow path that led past the house on the right. She took me by the hand and pulled me to a wooden gate behind the building. We passed it and Maria knocked energetically on a back door of the house: Tam, Tam, Tam Teram, Tam, Tam. I didn't feel particularly comfortable, but I trusted her and she gave me a reassuring nod. I heard a noise behind the door and soon a bolt was pushed. The door moved, and a fierce, sixty-something face with a stubbly beard pushed through the gap that had just opened. The beady eyes scrutinised me for a moment, then he looked at Maria and his mouth twisted into a broad laugh.
 "God bless you, Maria. I'm so glad you're still stopping by."
 "Hi, hi, it's all right David, this gentleman wants tea."

David looked at me curiously.

"This is Eric, give him your best tea, he's my guest."

David took me by the sleeve and gently pulled me through a dark corridor. On the left-hand side at the end of the corridor, dim light filtered through the cracks of a door. As we entered the room beyond, I saw that it was cast ghostly into the room by a peat fire, flickering red and illuminating a rough wooden table where six men were gathered. The youngest of them might have been seventy. They looked at me silently. David introduced me:

"That's Eric, he came with Maria."

They nodded in a friendly manner.
"Hello, Eric, I'm Eamon", "John", " Seán ", "Noel", "Seamus" and the last one introduced himself as James.

One of them pointed to an empty, armchair-like chair.
 "Welcome, Eric."

I sat down next to them. Maria and David, whom I had almost lost sight of in this strange atmosphere, also pulled a chair out of a corner of the room and sat down. Maria sat directly behind me without me noticing. She put a hand on my shoulder and turned to David:

"Bring Eric the tea, he's done me a big favour."
 "Sorry, the tea, of course."
 The men looked at me and nodded.
 "It was a nice day today," Seamus said, his last
incisor smiling at me.
 "Yeah, it was nice."

"Very nice," mused Seamus, "a bit of rain, but not
stormy," added Seán.

"We even had some sun today at lunchtime," John
added, "it was really warm."
 "It really could have been worse, couldn't it Noel?"
Eamon increased the possible weather that didn't
materialise.

"Yes, we've certainly had worse days," Noel
summarised. He sat opposite me and looked at me.
"You didn't pick the worst day for travelling."
 "Yes, it could actually have been worse." By now I
knew how to have these conversations.
 "Especially when you're picking up a hitchhiker at
this time of night."

Noel glanced at Maria and broke the rule of small
talk. I surmised that a story was being introduced,
and rightly so. David, the Landlord, turned to Noel
and spoke the entrée:
"Do you mean like when your father travelled from
Kinnegad to Moate? How long ago was that,

seventy years?"

"It was a completely different day to today, stormy all day, the rain fell as if the Lord God had sent us a deluge. I told you it was a completely different day to today. I was just nine years old, I know that for sure, it was the Saturday after my First Holy Communion. Yes, it's about seventy years now."
 Noel looked at the table, lost in thought, as if he could find the story there that had happened so long ago, a strange atmosphere. The others lowered their eyes in awe. Nobody said anything for the next few minutes, it seemed like a long time, but I didn't dare break the silence. The
gentle crackling of the burning peat in the fireplace emphasised the feeling in my stomach. I felt as if I had stepped into a conference that was not of this world.

"No, it really wasn't as nice a day as today, although the rain let up around nine, but it got even stormier."

Noel looked round and his friends nodded in agreement.
 "The wind was gale-force and you could hardly stand on your feet." So Noel was at least seventy-nine. He still had remarkably thick but snow-white hair for his age. He looked at me enquiringly.
 "I can't imagine a young man like Eric being

interested in the history of an old man."
 He was very wrong, or was he trying to make me particularly curious? I could hardly wait to find out what his story, which had
 been introduced with so much meaning in his voice, was all about. So I nodded encouragingly at him.

"Please go on, what happened back then?"

Meanwhile, I hadn't realised that a large cup of tea was already steaming on the table in front of me. Now David tapped me kindly on the shoulder: " Your tea," he said. I took a mouthful and almost choked, because this was a typical Irish tea - a stiff whisky grog, I should have known. It wasn't the first tea I'd been served in Ireland. I tried not to let my surprise show. Better prepared, I took another big sip from the cup. Noel's face twisted into a broad smile, his advanced toothlessness beaming back at me, only three lower and two upper incisors still visible. Satisfied, he nodded and began to talk:

Noel tells the story about his father

(1926)

As I said, it was a very stormy day. Dad was
supposed to be home at ten in the evening, but
he didn't come, not even at two or four, he didn't
come at all. Mum was in the kitchen all night. In
the morning she said to me and my two brothers
that she had to go to the Garda station in Moate
because Dad hadn't come home. As so often, I
was dragged into it because I was the youngest.
I don't think Mum dared go there on her own, so
she wanted me to go with her. She would never
have gone to the Garda station voluntarily, she
always said decent people had nothing to do
with the Garda. But it was an emergency and
worrying about Dad made her break her own
principles. Normally we would have travelled to
Moate with Betsy, our mare, but as she was
away with Dad, Mum asked her brother Dan,
my uncle, to take her there in the car. The
journey took about half an hour. When we
reached Moate, she gave Uncle Dan six shillings
so he could have a pint over at the pub and she
would run errands on foot. She didn't want to
tell him what she was up to, nor did he care in
the slightest. As a rule, he didn't let anyone tell
him what to do, but here he was happy to make

an exception and trotted obediently to the pub on the other side of the street; the unexpected windfall would keep him busy there for quite a while.

Garda Station was on Athlone Road and we still had about six hundred yards to go. When we reached it, Mum paused hesitantly in front of the entrance. She took me by the hand and looked anxiously at the door, then finally gave herself a push and pushed it open. We walked straight into a room and after a few steps stood in front of a kind of desk that stretched from one wall to the other. There were stacks of notes on it and a swinging door on the left-hand side. In the room behind it were several desks, some of which were occupied by uniformed Gardai officers. They looked up as we entered the room. With small hesitant steps, Mum walked up to the desk and one of the Gardai stood up and approached her. Was she okay, he asked kindly with a smile. Mum introduced herself as Nora McNicholas. He introduced himself as Tony Railey and asked what he could do for her.

"I'm looking for my husband Eamon."

"Eamon McNicholas?"

"Yes."

His face became serious, the other officers stopped their activities and looked over at us with interest.

Mum said that he hadn't come home the day before and wouldn't be home today either. Her voice sounded anxious, she had noticed the men's strange reaction. She told them that Dad had travelled to Kinnegad yesterday morning with the mare and the cart, to the spring market. He wanted to be back around ten that night. Mr Railey shook his head and asked if Eamon drank, maybe a little more sometimes.

Now Mum indignantly put her hands on her waist and vigorously said that by the testimony of Jesus Christ her husband was not a drunkard and she swore by the Blessed Virgin Mary that she had never seen her husband drunk.

The Garda had listened to Mum's incantations with an interested expression and turned to the swinging door, which he opened inwards. He asked us to follow him. Mum looked round at me uncertainly and I nodded as encouragingly as I could. By all the saints, I tell you, despite my young years, I knew she needed my support. I took her arm and pulled her after me. The Garda opened a door, turned to us and asked us to come in. He behaved very gently and smiled good-naturedly, he could probably empathise with how uncomfortable Mum felt in this situation. We followed him into a room that was about the same size as the one in the front. There were two large desks and a long bench against the right-hand wall. At one of the desks sat an elderly Garda, a dignified figure. There was another door on the opposite wall. Mr Railey stood next to the older man at the desk and spoke to him so quietly that I couldn't understand a thing. Every now and then they glanced over at us. After a while, the older man stood up and came over to us. He bowed gallantly to Mum and politely and kindly introduced himself as Sergeant Tom Flynn. He asked us to come over to him for a moment because he wanted to have a few words with us about Dad. He pulled a chair for Mum.

He told us that Dad was here because he had been banging on the outside door like mad at seven in the morning. The sergeant had just gone on duty and it was still locked. When he opened it, Dad grabbed the lapels of his jacket with both hands and started shaking them like a madman. He was Eamon McNicholas and begged for help. As if to emphasise the point, he shook it again vigorously. He invoked all the saints and begged for help.

As the sergeant did not recognise any immediate danger and Dad also had a distinct smell of alcohol, he thought it better to help himself first and freed himself from Dad's grip. This was, by God, hard enough because Dad had bear strength.

"Calm down Eamon," I said, "why don't you come in first, you're safe here."

He actually calmed down a bit so that he could take him to one of the cells without any problems. They had beds there for occasional guests. The sergeant pointed to the door that I had noticed when I entered.
 The sergeant asked Dad to lie down on the bed he had assigned to him. Dad followed without objection and the sergeant then placed a chair next to Dad's bed. He then asked him to tell him in turn what had actually happened. He then told him a story that was so unbelievable that he initially thought he was pulling his leg. But one look into his wildly flickering eyes, his unsteady breathing and other signs of his agitation told him that Eamon was certainly in no mood for jokes. The sergeant then believed that nothing could be done at the moment and that Dad needed a few hours' rest first. He then gave him

a powder that he himself occasionally took to calm him down. He actually fell asleep peacefully and decided to question
him again later in peace. He suspected that Dad had simply drunk more than he could handle. But the confused story still didn't leave him in peace, because it couldn't all just be a hallucination. Then the sergeant said it was probably time to wake Dad up. Perhaps it would be better if he told us everything himself, if he remembered it at all. Then he asked us to go next door, but paused and wondered whether it was good for me to see Dad in this state. Then he got up from the chair, I was a little scared because I didn't want to miss Dad's story. But my worries were unfounded because Mum said it was all right, I was a sensible boy. In fact, she probably didn't want to go to Dad alone with the sergeant. He took a key from one of the drawers and unlocked the door behind which Dad was. There were two barred cells in the room with the doors open. In one of them I recognised Dad on a cot, he was already sitting half upright and saw us enter. He looked dishevelled and tired. Mum ran to him and hugged him.

"Jesus Christ, what's happened to you?" she cried hysterically.

"Thank God you're here, Nora."

The sergeant then asked Dad if he could remember what he had told him that morning? I sat down at the foot of Dad's cot and waited anxiously.

And whether he remembered, as if you could forget something like that, but he didn't believe him.

To be honest, no, said the sergeant, as unbelievable as it all sounded. He might have bought the beginning, but then he'd just had one too many. The sergeant twisted his mouth into a broad grin, because even Gardai understand thirst.

Dad implored the Blessed Virgin Mary that he had experienced the story as he had told it, that nothing had been invented or left out. Dad was visibly upset.

The sergeant then suggested that it would be best if he told him again what he thought had happened. He would then make up his own mind. He had better leave the Blessed Virgin out of it, he was risking his salvation. He should only tell what happened that night. This would give him the opportunity to rethink his story and correct it where necessary. He was only interested in the facts, in what had really happened? The sergeant looked at him sternly.

"By all the saints," Dad began, "God knows I have nothing to correct, I assure you that everything happened the way I'm telling you now." He had calmed down, his gaze became thoughtful and he began:

Narrative of Eamon McNicholas

The market business was satisfactory, although it was rainy and stormy. I sold the chickens for a good price. I was completely sold out by around five in the afternoon. I ran errands at the market and as the day was successful and it was still very early, I decided to have a pint or two. I drank more like five and then made my way home. The rain had eased a little, but the wind had picked up. It was blowing directly in my face and Betsy was struggling to pull the car against the wind. My coat was buttoned up tightly and I had pulled my hat down over my face. We made slow progress against the wind. We must have been travelling for about an hour when Betsy shied. A few metres further on, in the faint light of the lamp, I recognised a female figure, ruffled by the

wind, who indicated with her hands that I should stop. I brought Betsy to a halt and recognised the face of an old woman who I estimated to be about eighty years old. I asked her what on earth she was doing on this dark road in this weather. She replied that she was visiting her sister in Kilbeggan and hoped the rain would let up a bit. She wanted to go to Moate and was actually good on foot, but in this storm it was very tiring and you could hardly beat it. Could I help an old woman and give her a lift part of the way? Of course I could help and even take her as far as Moate, as I still had a little further to go. May God bless me, she said. She introduced herself as Maria. With the agility of a young woman, she swung herself onto the wagon and sat down next to me.
I introduced myself and explained the reason for my journey. God should bless me, she repeated, and I was a good person. I was flattered and said I would be happy to help her. She tied her headscarf tighter and wrapped herself in her wide, black coat.
"A very stormy day," she said, "but quite nice."
"Yes, a nice day, stormy, but it could be worse."

"He really could," Maria confirmed. Then she didn't say another word until Moate. I had enough to do motivating Betsy to keep pulling the car into the wind. It was hard work, but we reached our destination.
She then interrupted her silence, telling me to stop there and she pointed with her bony index finger to the right to a large square in front of a pub, which was already closed. She was meeting friends there for a cup of tea and I was very welcome. A little rest would also do my good mare good. As I was feeling sleepy, this invitation came in handy and I gratefully accepted. It had been really nice of me to give her a lift and she nodded in confirmation. She tottered over to a gate to the right of the pub, pushed against it and it creaked open. She encouraged me to follow her. We stepped through the gate and Maria stopped in front of a door. Without hesitation, she banged her bony hand in front of it: Tam, Tam, Tam Teram, Tam, Tam. We waited. Then I heard a metal bolt being pushed and the door opened. The face of a man, I guessed him to be in his mid-sixties, became visible in the light of his lamp. He stretched out his arm to shine a light on Maria. Then he grimaced, which probably meant something like a

smile, and said: "Sláinte Maria. Welcome!"
She also replied with Sláinte Paul. Then he
lifted the lamp and shone it on me. Maria
introduced me. I had done her a big favour by
bringing her here in this awful weather, a nice
man. She had invited me to drink one of his
special teas, she hoped it would be okay. Paul
welcomed me and told me to come in and
keep them company. We followed him into a
room. Five old men were sitting round a
table, none of them under eighty. A peat fire
was burning in the fireplace and an oil lamp
on the table provided additional light,
flickering to show the shadows of the five
men on the surrounding walls. This wasn't the
taproom, it must have been one of the back
rooms. Paul introduced me to the five and
explained the occasion and that I would be
keeping them company that night. The old
men welcomed me one by one and
collectively invited me to join them. They
said the last thing as if in chorus and pointed
to an empty wooden armchair that stood at
the table with its back to the fire. I thanked
them and gratefully accepted the invitation.
Maria sat down in an armchair next to the
fireplace. Paul placed a large stone mug of
steaming liquid on the table in front of me; he

had drawn it from a copper pot hanging on a chain above the fire. It smelled like a stiff whisky punch. As I had got cold in the storm on the carriage, I gratefully accepted the mug and took a big gulp of the hot drink. The company murmured a sláinte to me, which sounded almost like 'Amen'. It was indescribable how pleasantly the hot liquid spread through my stomach and with a pleasant shiver I took another big gulp.

"Good stuff," I said, much to the satisfaction of the hosts.

"Hi Paul, Eamon likes your tea," then he turned serious.

The old man sitting opposite me asked me what was driving me out on the road at this time of night in this lousy weather. I told him about my day in Kinnegad.

But I had chosen a very unfavourable day for such journeys, this storm and today of all days.

I've travelled in storms before, it's not pleasant, but it works. Why should today be any different. The men looked at each other gloomily.

Did I really not know what night it was? The speaker looked at me with grey, deep-set eyes. I didn't realise what was supposed to be different about this night. I needed to fortify myself and took a stronger draught from my mug. I saw that Paul had topped up again. He really doesn't know, the speaker wondered to the others. "Unbelievable," murmured the group. The old people shook their heads in amazement.

"He doesn't know," muttered Paul, "good God."

 Then the speaker advised me to listen carefully.

"By the Blessed Virgin Mary, everything I tell you I know first-hand, for my ancestors were in the service of the O'Malaghlin for ten generations, whose dynasty ended with the death of the childless Saoirg O'Malaghlin in the 19th century. My grandfather was the last in their service, but the events have remained as vivid in my family as our own family history.

Today is the night of the eternal judgement of blood. For 350 years, this night has been repeated approximately every seventy years in the first storm after Easter. It is based on an event that dates back to 1505."

The night of the eternal judgement of blood

(1475-1505)

Moate was still a small town and the road from Kinnegad was more of a beaten track, trodden by the horses and feet of travelling merchants. Not far from here stood the house of Nuada O'Malaghlin, a wealthy landlord who had two grown sons and a daughter called Maria. His wife had died giving birth to Maria, and as he did not remarry, he offered his entire devotion to this daughter.

My blessed ancestor was employed by Nuada O'Malaghlin as a scullion fifteen years before Maria was born. By the time Nuada O'Malaghlin's wife gave her life, my ancestor had worked his way up to first butler and was running the clan's household. Maria grew up to be a beautiful maiden and my ancestor, Conchobhar (Conor) McClannard, was the closest confidant of the then twenty-year-old. He showed great empathy for the needs of such a young woman, and Conchobhar, himself only forty years old, was like a father or an older brother to her, depending on whose she needed. The time I am talking about was a hard time for the O'Malaghlins, as Maria's father had recently lost his eldest son in a hunting accident. Nuada O'Malaghlin had succumbed to self-pity, so it was especially important for the girl to have my ancestor Conchobhar at her side as an understanding friend.

The death of the eldest had turned the orderly succession of the O'Malaghlin clan completely upside down and the youngest had not been introduced to the obligations of a future clan chief. As is so often the case in such family constellations, the younger one cultivated a lavish lifestyle without the onerous obligations of a clan chief. It is fair to say that Jeremias, as the young man was called, was not exactly happy to be thrust into such an exposed role so abruptly. In short, on the day of his older brother's pompous funeral, Jeremias was already feverishly considering how he could let the chalice of the duties of a chieftain pass him by. He decided not to deal with this question for the time being and disappeared in the early morning of the day after the funeral without leaving

any news of his future whereabouts.
However, the missing gold coins from the
family treasure indicated that he was not
expected to return so soon. This gave
Mary the role of duty bearer, for Nuada
O'Malaghlin knew that Jeremiah would
not be able to carry this burden alone,
even if he did reappear in time. It was
certain that he would reappear one day. At
some point, the fortune he had taken with
him would be used up, and with Jeremiah's
lavish lifestyle, this was likely to happen
during Nuada O'Malaghlin's lifetime. Even
if Jeremiah was needed in the long term to
carry on the O'Malaghlin name, Maria
would still have to bear the progenitor
duties of the family clan. In other words,
Maria would manage the power and
wealth of the family until a worthy male
successor was up to the task. However, he
would first have to be fathered by
Jeremiah, and Nuada O'Malaghlin had not
yet given up hope that this would happen.
My ancestor thus took on the important
role of teacher, as Conchobhar had been in
the Prince's service long enough to know
what was important.
Maria took the task entrusted to her with

such seriousness that you would have to look a long time to find anything comparable in a person of such a young age.

You must bear in mind that this decision was inseparably linked to a great sacrifice for Mary, she had to commit herself to virginity for life, because if she had married in accordance with her status, not only would a large part of the family fortune have been lost for the dowry, Mary would also have had to contribute her strength to another family clan, so that she would no longer have been available for the task intended for her. But there was another reason that was even more serious. In order to administer the reign, Mary had to represent the dynasty to the outside world, and this was by no means a matter of course; on the contrary, such an endeavour was only possible in one form: Mary had to take a vow of perpetual virginity, so she had to become a nun. Only in this capacity would she be accepted by other clans and their followers, yes, even by her own followers, without a husband. Before she was twenty-one, Maria had travelled with her father on the long journey to Baile Àtha Cliath[1] to join a religious order there as a novice. When she was twenty-six years old, she took her perpetual vows in Baile Àtha Cliath. It had already been agreed at the time of her admission that she would then leave the order and return to her father's estate.

It so happened that clerical dignitaries frequently travelled the roads from Baile Àtha Cliath to the west, and so Mary placed herself in the care of two priests who had been ordered by the Holy Father in Rome to what is now the county of Longford. It was windy and rainy, but that didn't bother the priests in their closed carriage. They made good progress. In Kinnegad, Maria would have to separate from her companions to continue their journey to Moate. After two days' travelling, Maria and the reverends arrived here, and before they parted, they gave Maria their blessing. The wind had picked up during the day and the rain became heavier.

(1926)

---

[1] Dublin

The narrator paused and looked round. He extended the pause with relish, looked over at me and said to me:

"From here on, I'd better let Maria speak for herself, because she later confided what happened to my ancestor, who passed it down through the generations, so my grandfather told me the following."

Mary's story

(1505)

After saying goodbye to the honourable people, I went to the vicarage to spend the night there. The day was already well advanced and the priest might be able to organise a lift for the next day. To my disappointment, I found the vicarage locked and, as a nun, I didn't want to stay in an inn. So, without further ado, I decided to try my luck in another way. I knew that occasionally a carriage travelled from Kinnegad to Athlon, so I relied on God's providence. I set off on foot and left the main road for Longfort. I knew the way to Moate from my journey to Baile Àtha Cliath and it didn't seem to have changed since then. It was already very windy during the day, but as night fell, the wind grew into a snarling gale. It swept in from the west so that I could hardly fight it. The rain also seemed to have intensified, but a long coat with a hood gave me some protection. I must have been travelling for four hours. But it could have been less or considerably more, in a situation like this time cannot be estimated.

The roar of the wind was so strong that I only noticed the car when it came to a halt next to me. I couldn't see the driver, he was holding a lamp towards me, his face in shadow. He asked me why, as a consecrated sister, I was travelling alone on this dark path at this time of night. His voice sounded pleasant and I immediately felt trust in this person. This voice sounded familiar to me, as if I knew it. At the time, I believed in God's providence after he had tested me in that terrible storm, so I wasn't afraid to ask if he was travelling via Moate and could at least take me a good distance. The charioteer came to his senses and turned the lamp on himself. He said that he lived not far from Moate and introduced himself as the eldest son of clan chief Pádraig McLough, Seán

McLough. He said it was an honour to offer me a place at his side.
I recognised him by the light of his lamp and my heart tightened in his chest. Seán was a hunting companion of my brother's at the time, and he was even there when the accident happened. He, on the other hand, didn't seem to recognise me, at least there was no trace of recognition on his face. I thanked God that I didn't recognise him when he turned the light on me, because I could feel the blood rushing to my face, he should have noticed my blush. The last time I saw Seán, I was still fifteen and madly in love with him, but he'd barely given me a glance back then. It seemed that he hadn't actually looked at me, because he didn't recognise me and I couldn't have changed that much, or was it my Order attire?
I got on the buck with soft knees and was grateful for the darkness, my embarrassment would go unnoticed. Only now did I realise that I shouldn't have these feelings and tried to fight them. He's just an acquaintance, I told myself, nothing more. I'm a stupid brat, I kept telling myself, a little girl crush. I'm

twenty-six and a nun, the memory had overwhelmed me. I'm over that now. As if to prove it to myself, I asked him if he didn't recognise me. I was startled by the sound of my voice, for it was anything but certain and I hoped he hadn't realised in the roar of the storm. But his answer made my blood run hotter than ever.
He recognised me, of course, I was the daughter of Nuada O'Malaghlin. How could he not have noticed such a beautiful maiden back then? But she was now a consecrated nun and it would be unseemly to embarrass her. He had accepted that he had to make a strict distinction between then and now. However, feelings are all too often difficult to suppress. He knew, however, that he was no longer entitled to the feelings that were budding for me.
Now consecrated to God, I should no longer be desired for worldly love.
He had been madly in love with me at the time and my shy looks and the slight blush on my face when he looked at me had encouraged him to ask my father for my hand in marriage. As a descendant of an equal clan, it was nothing improper and he had of course asked his own father

beforehand, who would have approved the marriage with favour. My father, however, had behaved like a jealous suitor and brusquely refused. But then he changed his mind and told him that I wanted to consecrate myself to God and take eternal vows. His father himself was disappointed at first, but there was nothing to stop him consecrating himself to God. Both clans therefore remained on friendly terms despite the rejection.

Seán said he had deliberately not turned the light on himself at the beginning because he would have found it difficult to catch himself and didn't want me to notice. But now that I'd asked him so directly, he couldn't hold back any longer. How much he had hoped years ago that I would explain my motivation to him in person, that I would talk to him after my father had ruled out marriage. He would have been happy if he had been able to talk to me and perhaps I would have told him that I would have chosen him if I hadn't decided in favour of God. That would have been at least a small consolation for him, because he couldn't switch off his love for me.

Dark thoughts grew inside me. Seán had asked me to marry him, my father had never mentioned it, he hadn't even hinted at it. But then I came to my senses and calmly replied that my father had never told me, but it had certainly been too late and I could no longer think about my own future with the task it was my duty to take on. After my brother's fatal accident, I was the only one who could ensure the continuation of our clan, he certainly didn't want to confuse me. But then Seán said in astonishment:

"The death of Deaglán? No one was aware of the Lord's plan at the time. Your brother was still in perfect health when I presented my request to your father."

We had other plans, he said, I was too precious for marriage. At the time, Seán believed that the rejection was with my consent, but my ignorance of his proposal aroused an outrageous suspicion in us. My father had planned it for me from the beginning - without my knowledge. He had already decided on my virginity for life when Deaglán was still alive. As a nun, he would have me all to himself, no man would ever touch me. My father had

cheated me out of my happiness, betrayed and sold me out for selfish reasons. I realised in one fell swoop that he not only wanted to keep me tied to him for the rest of his life, he also wanted me to remain tied to him afterwards, never to be free for a man. Just as the feeling for my father, which had been fuelled by betrayal, broke down, the still smouldering love for the man next to me flared up again, more fiercely than ever before. I no longer resisted it, as I had done countless times. As a young girl, because I believed I meant nothing to him, in the convent, because it wasn't allowed. Hadn't God also been betrayed when I consecrated myself to him under false pretences? I hastened to tell Seán that I would not have chosen God, but him, without hesitation.
"Oh, Seán, my love."
But he replied:
"Honoured ones, it's too late, we can't change it anymore."
I told him that I had always loved him, from the very first moment and that I loved him now more than ever. If he didn't love me anymore, then I would give in.
"Me? Not love you? When I recognised

you, my love blazed more fiercely than before. Excuse me, honoured one, I must not, we must not, precisely because I love you ..., you, we must not, it is your salvation that is at stake. Eternal damnation awaits you if we give in to our weakness. You are consecrated to the Lord and we must not break that. If it were only about my own salvation, I would give it up to be allowed to love her, but we must not risk yours. I would be more wicked than your father if I were to accept your eternal damnation, pardon me, honoured ones, I must imprison my love, put chains on it so strong that it can never free itself again. That is the only labour of love I can still do for you. I can only ask you not to go to your father, his plan must not work out. Give your life to the one you have consecrated it to, our Lord."

My courage plummeted, was it really all over?

"Oh Seán, this cannot be what our Lord, Jesus Christ, wanted. What does he care about a person he got by deception? Didn't he bring us together himself, tonight, here in the storm. He could have sent thousands of others, but he sent you, his providence

brought us together."
"I fear you are mistaken, my beloved Mary, I believe Satan is leading us into temptation and we must resist it. He whispers in your ear that it is the Lord's providence, but in reality it is his own."
I replied that we should not underestimate the Lord. We made him a selfish and jealous man who demands agonising sacrifices from us, why should he do this? The Lord himself has given love and forgiveness. One cannot seriously believe that the Lord did this in order to deprive us of love and forgiveness afterwards. Is this wonderful, generous Christ on the other hand supposed to be the pusillanimous and malicious man who sends Satan to tempt us with our love of all things? I cannot and do not want to believe that. He himself had brought love to mankind. I was now completely convinced of what I was saying. I must have been blind all those years when I thought I was dedicating my life to God. I was blind because I closed my eyes so as not to see reality. I made my Lord small and ugly by forcing myself on him and proclaiming to the outside world that he wanted it that way. Because Seán

spurned me, as I believed, I had consecrated myself to the Lord. What someone else didn't want was supposed to be good enough for him? This is my real debt that I have to make good to our Lord? He will forgive me, perhaps he has already done so. I was a foolish girl whose eyes have only now been opened. I love this man next to me and our Lord gave me this love, now he expects me to accept his generous gift. I had to convince Seán that he would not jeopardise my salvation if he loved me, I was now determined.

The storm had become even fiercer and the horses were snorting with exertion. In this weather it was perhaps a good two hours to Moate and so I said to the man I loved next to me that it might be good if the horses and we ourselves took a breather for a while in the lee of the hut that had just appeared in front of us. In fact, however, I wanted to get rid of my religious garments. I still had my private clothes in my bundle that I had worn on the journey to Baile Átha Cliath, and my stature hadn't changed much since then. The robes of the Order were no longer mine to wear. The horses gratefully

accepted the respite and, on the pretext of having to do something, I apologised to Seán for a moment. When I returned after a while and the light of the lamp fell on me, I only heard a confused: "But!", then I put my finger to my mouth, indicating that I had something to tell him. I told him that I wanted to become his wife that very night. If he thought my salvation was at stake and therefore spurned me, I would not offer my spurned body to our Lord. Rather, I would give it to someone else, someone less than him, without love. I told Seán that he would rather risk my salvation by driving me into the arms of a man I did not love. If he didn't want me, someone else would have me. I was convinced that the Lord forgave me for this little trick, because I was helping the love he had given us to fulfil its right. Quietly and uncertainly, like a shy boy, Seán replied that no one else should have me, his resistance was gone anyway. I knew our Lord better than he did, but wouldn't it be better if I first became his wife before God?
"I will be your wife before God tonight. The only thing we can't expect is the

blessing of the church, but that's
dispensable. We make our promise before
God and he will bless us, there is no doubt
in my mind. He has brought us together
this night so that we can leave our
erroneous path. Why else has he kept the
doubt in my chest all these years? I have
tried to fight it, but it would not go away.
All my prayers have only made it stronger.
I tell you, and I don't feel the slightest
doubt about this, our Lord himself blesses
our love."
Seán had listened to me with wide eyes. I
had watched his face in the light of the
lamp and clearly saw the doubt leave his
face. At last he took me in his arms, held
me tightly and I felt his love overflow onto
me and mine too burst the dyke that had
held it in for so long.
After we had hugged each other like this,
entwined in our happiness for a small
eternity, I heard his muffled voice, free of
any doubts. We would be in Moate in
about two hours. There was a small inn
there and he knew the landlord very well.
He would give us a room and would not
mind if we were not married in the sense
of the church. He and his wife are good

and God-fearing people, but they don't get on so well with the priests. We would take our vows under their witness and drink a glass with them. Then we would become husband and wife, tonight, forever and ever, he promised me.

I also promised, and so we were engaged. The solemnity of the moment had made us forget the storm, which was now tugging at our carriage with increased ferocity, although we were reasonably sheltered behind the wall of the house. The horses snorted nervously in their harnesses. Then the storm calmed down again. It just seemed to be a particularly vicious gust, perhaps the devil raging about his defeat. Seán thought it would be better to continue on our way now, the horses had rested a little and were now becoming increasingly restless. A little later, they were struggling against the wind again. I was now leaning close to my lover, a large, thick blanket protecting us from the lashing rain. The storm and wetness didn't bother me, I felt better and happier than I had in years. It was as if love had erected an impenetrable protective wall around us. Time passed as quickly as the wind and

we soon reached the outskirts of Moate.
The wagon bumped along the stone-paved
road and soon Seán was steering the
carriage towards a house from which light
still flickered. He brought it to a halt in
front of a gate and asked me to wait a
moment. He disappeared into the house
through a door, but returned a few minutes
later with a sleepy-looking young man. He
introduced him to me as Torin, who would
look after our team. Fortunately, we didn't
have to get him out of bed. Leaning on his
arm, Seán led me into the house, through a
dark room into a back room lit by the
flickering glow of a fireplace. Sitting at a
large wooden table was a corpulent, good-
looking man, who looked to be about
thirty to forty, with a woman of about
thirty. She was a rugged beauty and I
guessed correctly, the landlord and his
wife. They kindly invited us to join them.
It wasn't difficult for me to greet them
with a smiling nod. Seán had already
briefly told them what we wanted and they
assured him that they would be very happy
to be our witnesses. The landlord officially
confirmed this with such a warm smile
that I wanted to give him a big hug. But

first we had to warm up and fortify
ourselves. The kitchen would be cold, but
there would still be plenty of bread,
cheese, ham and cake available. His wife
had risen in the meantime and poured a
steaming liquid from a large jug that had
been lying in the fireplace into
earthenware mugs, which she placed on
the table in front of us. Her own were still
full. His wife then disappeared into an
adjoining room, while the landlord picked
up his mug and wished the young couple
Sláinte. We took the hot mug in our hands
and as I lowered my nose into the vapour,
my inner self warned me to take a sip
carefully. Something hot, unfamiliar and
sweet at the same time ran sharply into my
mouth. I watched Seán and the landlord
drink less gingerly in large gulps. I could
see from their faces that the drink tasted
good, but I was fighting a nascent cough.
Then the brew reached my stomach and I
felt a sensation that explained the satisfied
look on their faces. I immediately slurped
a second, larger portion into my mouth
and let it pour into my stomach, spreading
a feeling of well-being. The cold and
discomfort of the weather had dissolved

into warmth and comfort. By the time I had emptied the cup, the ghost of my father had left me and completely dissolved; all I felt was pure love for my beloved. The landlord had topped up the drink when his wife pushed a large platter of delicacies onto the table. Only now did I realise that it must have been twenty hours since my last meal, so I didn't have to be asked twice to satisfy my hunger. A few hours must have passed and the landlord and his wife knew our story almost as well as I did. They listened attentively and did not interrupt our story, apart from the occasional honest indignation and unflattering remarks against my father and the clergy in general. After a brief pause for reflection, the landlord cleared his throat gently and then said that God had undoubtedly destined us for each other and we should make our vows here and now before them, his wife and he being our witnesses. He reverently lifted his belly out of the wooden chair and pulled his wife by the arm into the adjoining room. It wasn't long before they carried in a crucifix and a few candles, which they solemnly arranged on the table and the candles were lit. Then the landlord said that the celebrations were about to begin. The small congregation stood up and folded their hands. The landlord and his wife crossed themselves and we did the same. Then we solemnly recited the Lord's Prayer together, ending with the sign of the cross. They looked over at us with folded hands. I knew that everything else was now up to us. I had to go first, as I had to renounce an unlawful union. I had taken my nun's habit with me into the dark red flickering room in a suitcase. I solemnly took the suitcase, placed it on the table in front of me and opened it. I took out the robe and held it up so that it flickered like a shy ghost in the candlelight.

I said quietly and reverently, but with a firm, confident voice:

"Lord Jesus Christ. As a foolish, ignorant girl, I consecrated myself to you. I did it out of love and obedience to my father on the one hand, but also out of disappointment over a supposedly spurned love for a man on the other. Neither is worthy of you and if only I had had more sense, I would never have put you through

this. But you, in your infinite wisdom and goodness, never let the doubt in my heart go out, gave me the understanding to see through my error and finally sent me the one I love the most here on earth. I ask you to forgive me for presuming to be a worthy bride for you. I am convinced that even better women than I cannot be worthy. Before we ask you to bless my union with my mate, to whom I can be a worthy bride, I burn the wedding dress I should never have worn. You alone can look into my heart and know that I sincerely regret my mistake."
With these words, I grabbed the nun's habit and threw it into the fire. It burnt completely unspectacularly.
I was convinced that I was now freed from my foolish transgression and could ask God for the grace to bless my union with Seán.
With bowed heads, shocked faces and folded hands, the small congregation said "Amen".
We now swore an oath of eternal love and loyalty before God and sealed this with the sign of the cross and a final Amen.
Seán and I were now husband and wife,

given and blessed by God. What God has joined together, man shall not separate.
The host led us into the wedding chamber and we consummated the union given by God even before we were aware of it ourselves.
The night was full of love and passion, there was nothing I had to regret, everything was good and pure before God. But that night was to remain the only happiness I was granted in my life. I swear on my soul that God had nothing to do with everything that followed, apart from our child.
(1926)
The narrator paused; his expression was grim. "This is where Mary's story ends. Everything else was told to me by my grandfather, who knew it from his, and it goes back to my ancestor Conchobhar. What he didn't experience personally, Maria had confided to him.

Narrative of the ancestor Conchobhar McClannard

(1505)

Conchobhar McClannard himself was actively drawn into what happened, so deeply that he was never to be happy again for the rest of his life. I bear witness here to what people can do to other people. The lad who had looked after the horses and stabled Seán's carriage was a curious and talkative fellow. He had overheard what he saw as sinful goings-on that night. When he was sent out early the next morning on errands, Maria and Seán were still in their room. He told the first one about a devil's covenant that had been made in the house of his bread provider, in which a nun had sacrificed her robe to Satan in the fire.

As he was able to name the sinners, Mary's father, Nuada O'Malaghlin, and the Seáns, Pádraigh McLough, were personally alerted by the priest. A short time later, O'Malaghlin's and McLough's followers were on their feet. Nuada O'Malaghlin and Pádraigh McLough quickly agreed that the innkeeper and his

wife, who had long been suspected of being in league with the devil, were the villainous seducers. The priest agreed and said that it had to be established whether the poor children could still be rescued from Satan's clutches. He promised a favourable judgement and intercession, as he was keen to convict these devil's servants and, with God's help, save their poor victims from eternal damnation.
The clan chiefs and their entourage, the benevolent priest and a few dozen indignant 'righteous' Christians marched towards the inn of the innkeeper couple in the morning. Arriving in front of the wicked house, the priest crossed himself and sent a prayer of punishment against this portal to hell. He then struck the door of the house with his shepherd's crook and loudly demanded that all the occupants leave this wicked house. When the landlord stuck his head through the door, O'Malaghlin's men dragged him out. Some of the 'righteous' immediately pounced on the devilish landlord. But the priest stood protectively in front of him, both hands spread in the air, the shepherd's crook in his right hand.

"Stop," he shouted, "this is a case for the Holy Inquisition, only it can restore order." It has to be said that the Inquisition was practically inactive in Ireland, but locally there were always a few zealous advocates who called for it. The landlord's wife was also placed under his care, as were two maids and a farm labourer.

Nuada O'Malaghlin wanted to take care of Maria herself, but she and Seán had long since woken up from the general commotion. As they stepped through the door, they held each other tightly.

When the faithful saw this covenant of Satan in the flesh, they began to cry out loudly. They all knew that Mary had burnt the habit when this union was made. There was no doubt: it was a union of the devil. One of the Christians, who found it all unbearable, had picked up a stone and hurled it at the couple. It hit Mary on the forehead, causing blood to gush out. With a hissing command, Nuada O'Malaghlin sent a few henchmen against the stone thrower, who was beaten with long sticks until he lay on the ground and no longer moved. This all came as such a surprise

that the priest could not prevent it. Raising
both arms and pointing the shepherd's
crook towards the sky, he shouted:
"Stop, it is the business of the Holy
Inquisition. The lost couple is under the
protection of Holy Mother Church. No one
but the Holy Inquisition may judge them if
they are proven guilty. Eternal damnation
to those who anticipate the judgement of
the Holy Church."
The indignant ones calmed down, it is not
known whether out of fear of eternal
damnation or the bludgeons of the
O'Malaghlin henchmen. The bleeding
Maria and the tightly clutching Seán were
brutally torn apart by their own. No one
was ever to see the other again."
(1926)
The narrator paused for a moment, took a big
sip and lit a pipe, almost forgetting to smoke.
He drew in the fragrant smoke with relish and
then continued his story.
"It is not known what became of the
innkeeper, his wife and their servants,
whether they were consigned to some kind of
holy inquisition. Mary and Seán were saved
from this by the priest's intercession, after
both fathers had agreed on Mary's and Seán's

behalf to let him exorcise those confused by Satan. However, he demanded that Mary then return to her order and spend her life there. He was convinced that in this way she could escape eternal damnation.

 Nothing has been handed down about Seán's fate and my ancestor never heard from him again. There are various sources with different accounts of Mary's fate. However, I believe in the authenticity of my blessed ancestor Conchobhar McClannard's version.

(1505)

The days following the storming of the inn were hell for Maria. Her father preemptively assigned her the responsibility if the O'Malaghlin clan perished. My ancestor knew his clan lord well enough to know that he himself did not believe in the existence of a god and Maria's offence was not the work of the devil for him, but he saw it as an affront by his daughter against himself. She had betrayed the clan and deceived him. He only played along with the priest's theatre as far as it was useful to him. He would have liked to cut off the head of this good-for-nothing young McLough himself, but a feud with the McLough clan was the last thing he needed at the moment. The atmosphere in the O'Malaghlin house was irritable to the extreme. The priest's daily visits did nothing to improve the atmosphere; he seemed unable to wait for the exorcism. Maria fell ill in her grief, but did not dare to complain. Suffering and feverish, she lay in her chamber and Nuada O'Malaghlin had trouble convincing the priest that Mary's illness was of natural origin and not the work of Satan. The exorcism would have to wait until she had recovered. However, this condition dragged on for a long time and the priest had to be patient, which he found extremely difficult. One day, however, Mary's condition worsened so that they had to fear for her life. Now the priest could no longer be refused and insisted that the exorcism be carried out soon, because without it he would not be allowed to administer the Holy Sacraments of the Dying and Mary would be eternally damned.

Nuada O'Malaghlin could not afford to fall out of favour with the church and so, for better or worse, he had to agree. The priest insisted that the exorcism had to be carried out that very night, as there was a chance that Maria would not live to see the next morning. He instructed Mary to be laid out in the banqueting hall, in the centre of a pentagram defined by torches, with her head pointing to the top. This would ensure that once the devil had left the pentagram, he would not be able to return to Mary's body, as it was known that he was not allowed to enter the pentagram without authorisation. Only four people were to be present: himself, O'Malaghlin, my ancestor Conchobhar McClannard and the possessed woman herself. Everyone had to arm themselves with a crucifix, he would bring the large cross from the church and consecrated water. He only hoped that it was still the right time, but in the light of day an exorcism was not possible, he would pray.

The devil did not take Mary away prematurely and when the priest entered the house after dark, everything was prepared as he had instructed.

The banqueting hall had five entrances, none of which Satan was supposed to use. The priest personally arranged five consecrated candles on the doorsteps in

the shape of a pentagram, with the tips
pointing towards the inside of the hall. He
placed small bowls of consecrated water in
the centres. The large open fireplace in the
banqueting hall was intended as a gateway
for the devil, as he is attracted to fire. A
huge fire was lit in it. Once he had left the
house, he would not be allowed to enter it
again.

The large church cross was placed at the
foot of Mary in the pentagram. The priest
scrutinised everything once more with a
critical eye, then grumbled with
satisfaction. He had another stool placed
to the right of Mary, who was weakened
by fever. He ordered those present to sit
behind the large cross, outside the
pentagram. He instructed them to hold the
crucifix firmly with both hands in front of
their chests and not to let go of it,
whatever might happen. My ancestor
Conchobhar reported that he felt very
anxious. If it wasn't for the salvation of his
beloved Maria, God knows he would have
left the event, even if it meant losing his
position. He could only see cynicism on
his master's face, although he also
followed the priest's instructions to the

letter. He opened the ceremony by sprinkling consecrated water over Mary and praying the Lord's Prayer in Latin, then saying words in a language Conchobhar did not recognise. However, he reported that the atmosphere was tense to breaking point.

Maria suddenly opened her eyes and cried out loudly.

"That's Satan," the priest shouted excitedly and hastily sprayed large quantities of consecrated water over Mary, to which Satan reacted even more violently.

The priest muttered concerned words in Conchobhar's unfamiliar language and meanwhile rotated a rosary through his fingers. The devil looked madly at the priest through Mary's eyes and it seemed as if the priest was weakening.

"We have to burn him out," he shouted. He ordered her father to uncover her body so that he could perform the ritual. Conchobhar noticed Nuada O'Malaghlin's face change from cynicism to perplexity, embarrassment and then shame. He asked the priest if that wasn't going too far.

"Silence, you fool," the priest said angrily, "do what I told you to do."

Struck by these words, he turned to his daughter without resistance for the sake of his relationship with the church. He hesitated only briefly before opening Mary's nightdress.

The priest stared in horror at Mary's body, and the father also seemed to lose his composure. My ancestor recognised what had upset the men so much: Mary was undoubtedly carrying a child.

"It's worse than I thought," said the priest, "my power is at an end here. Only the Holy Inquisition can save her. She bears the fruit of the devil and I cannot exorcise her. She must be handed over to the Inquisition."

Nuada O'Malaghlin recognised his chance and took over again.

"I don't think that's necessary, Reverend. You yourself said that Maria was not a case for the Inquisition. You could get into trouble yourself if the Holy Inquisition were to find out about it. You know that I have my own options. I will take care of this Satanic scourge. But I'm counting on their help when it comes to my daughter's salvation again. I will send for her and everything will be prepared, just like

tonight, the devil will be her business again, I can't take care of that."
"You're right, my son," the priest replied uncertainly, "the Inquisition is ..., is always so thorough."
"That's what I mean," Nuada O'Malaghlin replied triumphantly, "they have enough to do as it is, it's good if we can take something off their hands."
 "Gentlemen," said the priest as he left the pentagram, "I await your call. I'll only take the large church cross with me, we'll certainly need the other one again very soon."
He hurriedly said goodbye and left the house.
The father ordered my ancestor to take Maria to her chamber, he seemed angry but said nothing more. When my ancestor Conchobhar asked Maria what had happened, the girl began to cry and laugh. Conchobhar was very confused, then Maria said that she was happy about the expected child, a child of love.
At this point, she told him the story that we have already heard from her mouth above.
"It's not the fruit of Satan?" he asked

cautiously.
"My dear, dear Conchobhar, it is a child of love, from a blessed union before God."
Maria's illness seemed to have blown away, and indeed, her thoughts were only centred on how she could save her child, and Conchobhar would help her, that was for sure.
"It's going to be very, very difficult, I believe you because I know you better than anyone. You're clever, and I've never heard you talk about our Lord the way you did. But it seems right to me, it sounds right, it feels right. For God's sake, my child, we have to find a way."
There was no way!
Maria blossomed. She seemed to have recovered from her illness. She was happy about her child, and happiness excludes illness.
 Then a woman came to her and said:
"We can do it."
This woman came again and said,
"We have to look at it."
She pressed Maria on her stomach and did other things that Maria neither understood nor liked.
"We'll sort it out," the woman said again

and disappeared.

My ancestor, Conchobhar, was sceptical, but knew nothing definite. Then Nuada O'Malaghlin sent him on an errand to Galway. My ancestor didn't like it at all, he didn't want to leave Maria alone, but he had to obey.

The woman came to Maria a few days later, dissolved liquid from a vial in water in a cup and gave it to her. Maria hesitated, but the old woman reassured her:

"It will do you good, you don't need to worry. You'll get some sleep afterwards, then everything will be fine, drink, your father ordered it."

"I'm just going to sleep on it?"

"It's a wonderful sleeping elixir, after which everything will be fine."

Maria complied. She said that she felt strange after taking it. When she woke up, something had changed. She felt terrible pain in her abdomen, but that wasn't what was bothering her. Something was missing, she could feel it. She didn't yet know what was missing, but she was gripped by the kind of panic that comes from an uncertain danger. Overpowered

by an irrepressible feeling, she began to scream. Then Conchobhar appeared in her room, deathly pale and confused.
"Something's happened to me," she cried fearfully, "I don't know what, but it's terrible!"
Conchobhar began to weep, although it was not proper for a man to do so in those days, shaking violently with grief. Maria forgot her own grief for a moment when she saw her friend in such despair.
"What have they done to you?" Maria asked sympathetically.
"Me?! It was done to you and I let you down. I should have known, I should have refused to go. I was sent away from you on a fool's errand. They wanted to get rid of me so that I wouldn't stand in the way of this shameful deed. I feared for my position. They didn't tell me, but I should have known. You can't forgive me for that, I can't forgive myself for that. I should never have left."
"What didn't they tell you?" Panic gripped her, she suspected what had happened, but she didn't want to admit it, it was too cruel.
"I have abandoned you, my child, perhaps

God can forgive me, but no human being
can, I cannot forgive myself."
"What?" cried Maria, "what's happened?"
By saying it, she realised that she had been
aware of it all along. She didn't want to
admit it, deny it, as if that would undo it.
"What has happened to me? I can no
longer feel my child."
She clasped both hands in Conchobhar's
skirt lapels.
"Say it's not true!"
Resignedly, Conchobhar whispered:
"It's true, it's the bloody, cruel truth, I
didn't stop it."
Maria let go of Conchobhar, she could
barely hear what he was saying. He was
no longer acquitted by her. Her body sank
powerlessly into the pillows. Her eyes
stared blankly at the ceiling.
(1926 at the inn)
The narrator leaned back and paused, taking
several strong puffs from his pipe, then
continued:

The curse

(1505)

Mary's dead body was found in the Shannon, nobody knows how she got there, the river flows many miles away from Moate.

Killing yourself was a mortal sin. There were many voices, as the event caused quite a stir at the time. A public enquiry was called by the Athlon court. The church had its own enquiry. Although Nuada O'Malaghlin would have preferred to put an end to it, he was unable to prevent the uproar despite all his influence. For the officials, the case was soon over; a case of suicide was of no further interest to them. Maria's body was handed over to her father soon after Moate. He was informed on the same day that her body was not to be buried on consecrated ground. The priest demanded - and he was not alone in this - that her remains be cremated because they posed a danger to God-fearing people.

Nuada O'Malaghlin refused to burn the body of his beloved daughter. An attempt by the righteous Christians to rise up was crushed by the henchmen of the O'Malaghlin clan. He would behead with his own hands anyone who even began to harbour such a desire. Mary's body was buried uncleaned on the O'Malaghlin estate. The circumstances were clear to the faithful:

A nun had been impregnated by the devil under the influence of two witches (the innkeeper and his wife). Nuada O'Malaghlin, himself possessed by the devil, had prevented Mary from being handed over to the ecclesiastical court. The fruit of Satan had been removed from Mary's body by himself and no one knew what had become of the devil's bellows. By killing herself, Mary had sacrificed herself to her husband, Satan. According to the church, Mary's body had to be handed over to the purifying fire in order to avert harm to the village. But this was thwarted by the devil's vassals, her father. The people knew that the matter was not over, the witch (Mary) would claim her victims.

Now it is well known that the devil is a cynic. Nothing happened for a long time and the memories of these events faded,

although they were not forgotten. The prodigal son of the O'Malaghlins did indeed return home. He found a wife. The O'Malaghlin clan remained intact and the son of the returnee had long since reigned and the events that followed were reported by Conchobhar's grandson.
(1570)
The events surrounding Maria's sacrilege were almost forgotten. No one remembers the occasion, but one day James O'Malaghlin, the then lord of the clan, had the body of his Aunt Maria exhumed. He was struck by lightning: Maria's body was completely intact, with not a trace of decomposition to be seen. He was completely mesmerised by the beauty of this woman, who was his aunt. Something inside him whispered that this could only be the work of the devil, but like his grandfather, he was not a great believer in God. So he preferred to believe in natural causes that had preserved his aunt's corpse so perfectly. He fell in love with the image of this woman; he had never seen a more beautiful one in his life. But Maria's body deteriorated within a few days of her exhumation. The last time he saw her, she

looked like an eighty-year-old old woman. This image haunted him and the image of his beautiful aunt kept intermingling with it. It took some time before he found something like peace again.
(1575)
One day, many years later, he was on business in Kinnegad. As he made his way home, the strong wind of the day was already a full-blown storm, rain lashing through his face. He must have travelled a few miles when he recognised the figure of a woman by the side of the road. The closer he got, the more he realised that she must be quite old. When she noticed him coming, she stood in the middle of the path and forced him to stop.
My ancestor, Conchobhar's grandson, received no information about what happened next. His master was found the next day in a terrible state.
His return had been expected late that night. But when neither he nor any news of him arrived the next afternoon, my ancestor became worried and sent people out to look for him. In the evening, they received a tip-off from a farmer who claimed to have seen him. It was late at

night when they found him. He was lying in the dry stubble of a bog[2] , not far from the inn where his aunt and Seán had their mysterious wedding. His carriage lay overturned in the field half a mile away and the horses were not found until the next morning. His people thought he was dead at first, he was lying there motionless. His face looked as if it had been frozen in horror. It must have been something terrible, no-one had any idea what had happened to him. He didn't say a word for a long time, but people talked, at first furtively behind closed doors. A connection to the earlier events was quickly established, as people knew about the O'Malaghlins' involvement, and the proximity to the cursed inn did the rest. One afternoon he suddenly heard his master calling in a fever:
"It was her, by God, it was her. I recognised her."
Then after a few seconds he shouted:
"Maria!"
James died on the same day. The mysterious events surrounding James

___

[2] Irish peat field

O'Malaghlin preoccupied people and the Church. The case of Mary was brought to the fore again and was soon considered "solved":

The devil had waited seventy years until he had taken his first victim after the sacrilege, the circumstances did not allow any other conclusion. The unredeemed Mary returned for her blood sacrifice. But the death of these poor victims was not the worst of it. Anyone who fell into Mary's trap was doomed to eternal damnation. She took revenge for her dead child, this spawn of Satan. But perhaps she had also quietly nursed this brat after giving her life to the devil, remember: the foetus was never found.

Time ate away at the memory of these events, and they would have faded long ago if another mysterious death, comparable to that of James O'Malaghlin, had not occurred almost exactly seventy years later.

(1645)

A stranger was travelling in a wagon from Kinnegad to Moate. Eyewitnesses said they recognised an old woman who had got into the stranger's wagon. What is certain is that the stranger's body was found near Moate, not far from his wagon, and it was stormy and wet. Again, this case was investigated by the church. No signs of murder were found by the official investigating officers from Athlon. A natural death was declared without further ado.

(1926 in the inn)

The people of Moate knew better:

Every seventy years or so, the damned Maria opened a blood judgement in which she demanded retribution for her dead child. The victims of this blood court were unsuspecting travellers who, on a stormy, rainy spring night, picked up an unknown old woman in their carriage, just like Seán Maria. Only it is not a young, charming woman like them, but an old woman. This curse could never be ended, because after Maria was exhumed, no one ever saw her body again, let alone had the opportunity to place it in the purifying fire!"

The narrator paused, inhaled the pipe smoke. "There is nothing to prove that this judgement of blood really existed or exists, but the devil is cunning and always makes us forget. The Eternal Blood Judgement will

exist until the end of time, unless the unlikely event occurs that Mary and her aborted baby undergo purification by fire together. If anyone takes this wretched Mary with him in his chariot, he is doomed to death and his soul will be consigned to eternal damnation."
Hours must have passed by now. None of those present said a word, only the fire crackled eerily in the fireplace. The old man's story had planted a feeling in my stomach that I had never experienced before in my life. I hardly dared to look at one of them. Only after a while did I lift my head and let my eyes wander cautiously round the room. The old people were sitting quietly and motionless in the circle and there was already an air of death hovering over them all, at least that's how it seemed to me. Only now did I realise that Maria was no longer in the room. The silence weighed heavily on me, the crackling from the fireplace was no relief. When I could bear it no longer, I decided, taking heart, to break the spell and turned to the narrator.
"There must have been other victims if their stories are true."
My question thawed the old man, because his face, which had been like a death mask a few

seconds before, filled with life again:
"Oh yes," he burst out and continued the
frozen ritual of tamping his pipe. I didn't push
him, because I was happy about the life that
was now awakening in the room. Only when
he had his pipe ready for use did he say as he
scrutinised it:
"There have always been strange deaths
here."
He put the pipe in his mouth and took a chip
from the fire to light it again. He inhaled
three strong puffs and then continued:
"What almost all the cases have in common is
that the circumstances were not publicised.
The events of 1505 were always suppressed,
nobody liked to remember them, but every
abnormal death brought them back to
people's minds again and again."
He inhaled the smoke again, so I dared to ask
him a question:
"I live here too, why haven't I heard anything
about it?
" "You're a stranger here," said the old man.
Something inside me rebelled.
"Me? Our family has lived in Rossmore for
many generations, it should be close enough
not to be a stranger."
"Sure," he replied, "I don't mean foreign in

the usual sense either, your family only started to put down roots here a few generations ago. These unfortunate things are only passed down from generation to generation and are only talked about within those whose ancestors were already rooted here at the time."
When I tried to say something back, he waved me off brusquely and continued unabated:
"I said there was almost no information, but I heard about one case that is said to have happened. It was the last one I knew of. It happened at a time when my grandfather was still alive. It may be that some people know more about earlier cases, but people don't like to talk about them openly. My grandfather told me about a case that happened in 1856, and the uncanny thing about it is the similarity of the events.
(1856)
A stranger from Dublin, who had been travelling for two days, had wanted to take a day's rest in Kinnegad. As it was very windy during the day and heavy rain started in the afternoon, he visited an inn to pass the time. The wind escalated into a storm and the rain subsided, although it continued to spray

lightly but constantly. It must have been the alcohol, but around seven in the evening he suddenly decided to continue on his way to Galway, which was his destination. He set off in the direction of Athlone. He may have been travelling for two or three hours when he saw a hooded figure standing by the roadside in the light of his lamps. He reined in the horses and saw a wrinkled face peering out of a cloak in the lamplight. It was that of an old woman. He asked her what she was doing here so late in this weather and told her as best he could, for the alcohol in him made it difficult to speak. Almost inaudibly, because the howling of the wind almost drowned out her voice, she said she was on her way to Moate. He thought of his old mum sitting at home in front of her old fireplace. He imagined her standing here as miserable as this old woman and offered her a lift, it was on his way. He told her that she would feel the wind here too, but it was always better than walking.

She didn't need to be told twice, she climbed onto the trolley as nimbly as a monkey and sat down next to him.

"Thank you son, in Moate I'll take you out for a proper nip with friends."

Then she asked him if he wasn't worried about taking a stranger with him in this darkness and storm, and giggled softly.
 The stranger laughed out loud:
"I don't think you'll do me any harm." He laughed out loud again.
"Certainly," said the old woman, "certainly, son."
 She giggled once more and fell silent for the rest of the journey, which dragged on doggedly against the storm. After a few hours, they nevertheless arrived in Moate, the old woman showing no sign of fatigue. She hopped nimbly off the trestle, and if he hadn't seen her old face, he would have mistaken her for a young thing.
"Come on, son," she said as they arrived at what looked like an inn, "we know which inn it is, of course."
The narrator chuckled now too. He took some more of the pipe smoke and continued his story:
"The old woman ran to a door and pounded on it with her fist, a force he would not have believed this scrawny figure capable of. It didn't take long for the door to open. A man peered through the gap and the old woman whispered something, then signalled for him

to come in. Before he could object, she said
that the servant would take care of the horses
and cart.
They led him into the room you already
know. A lively fire was raging in the open
fireplace. In the centre of the room stood a
large oak table at which four old men were
sitting. He was shown to a seat and sat down.
As soon as he was seated, he had a large mug
in his hand, which he recognised as whisky
punch. He quickly slurped down the soothing
brew. The old people looked at him lurkingly,
sitting there motionless and silent. After a
while, the old woman came to him and
pressed a new punch into his hand.
"Drink, son, it will do you good!"
After a period of silence, he might already be
holding his fifth punch in his hand, one of the
old men suddenly broke the silence:
"Do you know what night it is?"
The stranger didn't understand, but the old
man didn't wait.
"Tonight is the night of the eternal judgement
of blood, my poor brother."
The stranger still didn't understand, he was
probably too drunk.
"You don't have to understand anything
either, my little son," he heard the old woman

say behind him, "my child couldn't understand it either."

The last thing the stranger noticed were the four old men. It seemed to him as if four dead men were sitting there. Before he lost consciousness, he heard the voice of the speaker:

"You belong to us now, you are the fifth child of Mary."

The stranger must have come round again," said the narrator, "because he reported what happened. We don't know exactly who he told about what happened. What is certain, however, is that his dead body was found the next day towards evening, not far from here. The horse and cart had disappeared and never reappeared."

Silence spread again in the flickering of the fireplace. The angel of death filled the room again.

(1926 Garda station)

"I'm not a fool," my father said and I saw him shaking all over, "God knows I'm not. I recognised the role I had fallen into. In seventy years' time, I would be sitting at that very table and there would be six of us. I would have to witness one of us telling an unfortunate man about the night of eternal judgement and condemning him to bring a seventh into our company in another seventy years. I sat at the table of the damned and tried not to let my fear get the better of me. My head was pounding like a steam engine. Maria was cursed to lure another victim every seventy years. The victims were supposed to be about the same age as her child, if she had grown old with him in a peaceful life. Her child was the spawn of Satan, people say. I don't know if it's true. But I also know that unbaptised babies are damned. It all seems to be a cynical game of the devil.

I didn't go along with it. You have to imagine the unbridled fear that raged inside me. My life, no, my salvation was at stake. You know that I am a righteous man and no more sinful than any normal person. I didn't want to be drawn into this evil plot of the devil and as a good Christian of the Holy Catholic Church I should be able to evade Satan. I withdrew from the party of the damned and left all the aged dead foetuses behind. Without saying a word, hounded by the devil, I left the damned inn and ran for life and salvation for all I was worth. Behind me I heard the screams of the dead children. I didn't let anything stop me, how could I in my panic. You wouldn't believe how happy I was when I saw the policeman outside the station. You know the rest, but by all the saints, pray for me. I don't know if I've really escaped the curse."

My father's whole body was shaking. He kept calling out:

"Pray for me, my strength is not enough."

My mum crossed herself and pushed me roughly:

"Pray for your father."

She also seemed agitated, only the policeman said that father had simply had too much to drink and was fantasising.

The sad end: my father died the same week. It was very difficult for us. We were sure that Mary had taken her sixth victim. We concealed the circumstances of his death so that he could be buried in consecrated ground. We knew that the church would never allow a damned person to be buried. There was nothing official about the circumstances of his death.

Mum was also convinced that he would escape damnation in consecrated ground. After all, he hadn't brought any personal guilt upon himself."

Epilogue

Old Noel ended his story here. The landlord poured our cups full of that wondrous tea again. I must admit that I was deeply impressed by his story, although of course I never believed it was true. However, the eeriness of the room and the stories did not fail to have an effect on me either. I couldn't escape a certain sense of trepidation. I had already heard a lot about the storytelling skills of the Irish, and I have also experienced a number of storytellers. But this one surpassed them all. The silence was icy. I said to myself. That's part of their game. But I don't know why I believed the storyteller more than myself. After quite a while of silence, Maria suddenly broke the silence:

"It's getting late," she continued, turning to me:

"You'd better stay here tonight, it'll be better travelling in the light tomorrow."

I felt reluctant to spend the night in this house, then I called myself to order. It's difficult to return to normality after a story like that. It's like after a nightmare. Then Maria said:

"You can spend the night in the bridal suite," she giggled loudly.

"Very funny," I said.
 She said a little more matter-of-factly:

"It's the only decent place to stay here in this house."

"I don't care where I sleep."

"Listen, listen," shouted one of the old men, "the seventh doesn't care where he spends the night."
 The men and Maria laughed out loud at my expense. Maria was the first to speak up again: "Come on, son, I'll show you the way."
 This little son made the blood in my veins freeze, briefly, then reason tried to regain the upper hand. I got up and followed Maria, who was already moving.

"Have a good and peaceful night," I heard the scornful voice of the previous narrator."

"Yes," shouted another, "we would be delighted to see you in our circle again."

The clique laughed unrestrainedly. That night I dreamt of the scaffold. I was the delinquent and had been sentenced to death by the council of six old men. I saw Maria, young and beautiful, wearing the robes of a religious order.
 "Come, my beloved," she said, "let us beget a devil."

Although I was attracted to this woman, I did everything I could to resist her.

"I don't believe in the devil," I shouted.

"Well," she said, "then what's holding us back."

"All the dead children," I shouted, feeling panic.

"You don't have to be afraid, my love," she said, but her voice sounded as if I shouldn't trust her.

Suddenly the beautiful woman turned into an ugly old woman. Her voice called out:

"Come, my love, I want a child from you."

"So you can kill it," I screamed, yes I screamed.

I was suddenly in a tight cage. A voice said:

"He must not be born, he is the fruit of Satan."

I saw a big disgusting hook coming through an opening, I was going to be aborted.
"I'm not what you think I am. I'm just a normal foetus."
But the abortion tool came mercilessly closer.
"No," I shouted, "I would become a normal child, why don't they want me?"
Then this thing grabbed hold of me, drilling into my womb.
"No," I shouted, "no."

***

I woke up and lay in my bed, drenched in sweat. The old narrator from the previous night was leaning over me.

"You were dreaming," he said.

"Yes," I said, gradually coming round.

"Your stories, my God ...   In my dream, I was the next victim in the clutches of Maria, you understand, that Maria."
 The old man smiled.

"But my boy, I told you yesterday when you came to us that it wasn't raining or storming. Above all, it's September, there's no blood court."

Even in the morning, he did not deviate from the fact of the existence of an eternal judgement of blood.

The storyteller from Donegal

It's a storytellers' festival weekend as we await Donegal storyteller George O'Flaherty in Joyce's Bar. It would be my first time seeing and hearing him, but everyone else here knows him. George always tells very special stories that are more fairy tales than stories that actually happened or could have happened. But the Irish love fairy tales and are convinced that there is a kernel of truth in them. I share this passion with them and therefore eagerly await George and his stories.

Then a tall heavy man enters the bar and from the reaction of those present I easily guess that it is George, he may be about 50 years old, maybe a few more or less. He walks straight to the bar and greets Anny Joe, whom I no longer need to introduce, with a warm hug. With George's stature and little Anny Joe, I just hope he doesn't crush her. Anny gives him her lovely little-girl smile, so I can rest easy about that. Afterwards, he moves without hesitation to the raised chair in the centre of the room and sits down on it, he knows his way around here. Nobody has to ask for silence, it comes naturally.

"I'm glad you're all back, then the last story I told here can't have been so bad after all."

His voice is exactly as I expected given his stature, it has a sonorous bass.

"I also see a few new faces and hope that those who lured you in here don't embarrass themselves today." He has to laugh at that himself. Although he hasn't looked at me, I feel addressed.

"Well," he continues, "today I would like to start by telling you about a profession that unfortunately seems to have died out. It's the profession of a dream designer."

The dream designer

In those days, when people still had dreams, there was a special kind of artist. He was the only dream designer far and wide. The fame of his art extended far beyond the country's borders, and what's more, his fame transcended space and time. So it was no wonder that this fame reached right up to the present day.

In this present, there are no more dreams, and what people think are dreams are nothing but illusions. In this dreamless present, there is a man who distrusted illusions but did not realise that illusions are not dreams. He lived in the sea of possibilities, but the pull of illusions is too strong for him to grasp any of them.

The fame of the dream designer reaches his ears. At first it is just a fleeting breeze, one of the elements from the sea of possibilities. But this gentle breeze turns into a storm and he suddenly realises that his illusions are not dreams. He decides to seize this one opportunity to create a real dream for himself. He whirled through the maelstrom of time to land where the famous artist worked. He immediately sought him out to have a huge dream created. But it wasn't that easy to hire the dream designer. When the man from the present went there, the artist was extremely uninterested.

"You are not qualified to have me create a dream for you. Go and acquire the necessary qualifications."

The man from the present asked how they could be acquired. But the artist replied:

"You have to find that out for yourself, it's part of the qualification." The man was already thinking about travelling back to his world of illusions, because you don't have to qualify for illusions. But then the man came to his senses and said to himself:

"Have I been drifting around in nothingness for so long", as the sea of possibilities was called, "to capitulate here at the first difficulty?" The man from the present decided to acquire the necessary qualification. However, as he did not yet know what he had to do, he asked one of the artist's journeymen. He said:

"The qualification is unspeakable, but I will give you one piece of advice: look for the blue flower and bring it to me."

Now the man from the present was more perplexed than ever. So he asked the master's apprentice about the blue flower. But the apprentice said:

"You can't find the blue flower because the garden in which it grows is not of this world. But I can give you some advice. The blue flower must find you. When it has found you, bring it to me."

The man from the present found his task more difficult than ever before. So he set out in search of the blue flower that could not be found, the flower that was supposed to find him. He wandered for days and weeks, crossed hills and travelled through valleys, asked the country and its people about the blue flower, but no one could give him any information. So one day, exhausted, he came to a small farmhouse. His only wish was to rest. With the last of his strength, he knocked on the door and the door opened, but no one had opened it. With no strength left to continue his journey, he entered the house and found a table laid for him. He was hungry and sat down to partake of the plentiful bread, meat and wine. When he was full and his thirst quenched, he went into an adjoining room and found a bed made up. He still thought that all this could not be true, but he was too tired to get to the bottom of it. So he went to the bed to stretch his tired limbs. It only took a few minutes and he had fallen into a deep sleep. And then he dreamt that the door to his bedchamber opened and a young woman came to his bedside. He could not recognise this woman, and yet he could not help thinking that he knew her. The harder he tried to recognise this woman, the more indistinct she seemed to him. But then he took heart and asked her about the blue flower. All of a sudden, he saw her clearly in front of him.

"I have waited so long for you, my love," she said. And indeed, her face shone out of a beautiful flower whose bright blue colour dazzled him, but he could no longer take his eyes off her. She was standing in a meadow with many wonderful flowers, but for him there was only this one, and picking it was his most fervent wish.

He awoke from his sleep and knew that his blue flower had found him. He hurried back through valleys and over mountains to rush joyfully back to the master's house. He thanked the apprentice for his advice, but told him that he could not give him the blue flower. He met the journeyman and told him the same thing. Then he stood opposite the master, who smiled. He took the master's hand and, with tears in his eyes, told him: "
Master, I thank you above all for this wonderful dream."
But the master raised his hands in a placating gesture and said: "
You created this dream yourself, I was only your helper. Bring the blue flower back into your world and reality will be the most successful design of your dream."

***

"Perhaps there are one or two people here who are just as happy as the hero of my story because they too have found their blue flower," the storyteller concluded.

Haiku

The unity of
being between birth and death:
The Time and its space.
***

The last secret rests
forgotten in the cold wind
let 's you float and fly.
***

Where happiness wins,
death can no longer prevail
wickedness loses.
***

Only your heart knows
the true nature of being
your own source of life.
***

A grey rainy day
kindles in me a longing
for a new true love.
***

Wisdom flies over
the edge of the horizon,
gateway to heaven.

The survivor

I once knew a man," George begins his second story, "who was very confident in his ability to recognise potential dangers in advance and prepare for them. He had some survival strategies and had demonstrated them in survival camps or in individual actions. But even greater than his abilities themselves was his ego and the resulting craving for recognition, so that - if you were a therapist - you could have deduced that he had a huge profile neurosis. I'll call this man David for once. I want to show you with my story that you can't plan everything."

* * *

David never travelled without a neoprene suit when using the ferry between Holyhead and Dublin after the Estonia disaster.
 It doesn't get that cold in the Irish Sea in winter, but surviving more than half an hour in the water without this suit is practically impossible. How right David is.

It's January and even in Ireland it's a few degrees below zero. Despite the Gulf Stream, the Irish Sea is barely more than four degrees.
 It all happens very quickly. No more than 30 minutes have passed between the first

irregularity and the total sinking of the ferry.
Death comes almost undramatically. Most of the
few hundred passengers don't even make it to
one of the lifeboats. They are pulled directly into
the depths with the ferry. The ninety people who
have launched a boat with some of the crew and
are hopefully sitting in it are also caught up in
the whirlpool a little later and all of them are
pulled into the depths. Of them, only David
resurfaces because he still has a lot of air stored
under the rubber of his suit.

When he realises his situation, there is not much
or anyone left of the ferry. Of the few remnants
of the "Irish Future" still floating around, only a
white lifebuoy attracts David's attention. As the
water penetrating his suit makes it more
strenuous to stay afloat, David paddles towards
this lifebuoy. He feels good under the
circumstances; he is warm and can still think
clearly. Despite the stormy sea, he reaches the
ring and hangs on.
To be on the safe side, he had previously
calculated that he would survive for at least
twenty-four hours if the worst came to the worst.
The prospects are therefore more than good, as
the Irish Sea is not exactly one of the least
travelled waters. Even if no distress call was

made from the ferry - which is unlikely - it will be missing within two hours of sinking. In all likelihood, the rescue teams are already on their way and it is only a matter of time before they discover it.

David is proud of his foresight, which made him put on this five-millimetre-thick protective skin. Amused, he thinks that freezing to death will not be the cause of his death. A kind of lust comes over him when he thinks of the headlines in the "Irish Times", which will report on his clever survival strategy in the next few days.
 A few hours in the darkness of the Irish Sea seems a small price to pay for the publicity he can expect from the media, having been an experienced survivor of many expeditions in the South American jungle.
 Not that David is unconcerned by the many deaths in this catastrophe. He is already thinking about the brother and sister who offered him vinegar crisps from a bag. At the nascent thought that these lovely children are now dead, he switches his brain off for a moment.

He succeeds in focussing his attention back on his idea of the expected jostling reporters in the foyer of the Shellborn Hotel, to whom, depending on their sympathies, he will reproach one or two chunks of experience from his odyssey in the Irish Sea. He will look modestly but confidently into the camera when the Irish broadcaster RTE shoots the report.

 The young woman from Kerry comes to David's mind. How old was she, sweet twenty-one. She was on her way to a three-week holiday. In her younger years, she had already become the manager of a branch of an Irish pub chain in Germany. Fiona had dark, sparkling eyes. Despite her career, she had remained the simple country girl. Her white laugh was enchanting - and David was mesmerised. They had fooled around at the bar and David had promised to visit her in Frankfurt in February. He had been a little enamoured.

David is almost glad that he is cold at this moment, despite his thick suit. The idea that his life could be in danger makes him choke down the lump in his throat, the lovely girl is dead and he is no longer thinking about it.

It was a different story when he had to survive eight days in the Brazilian jungle alone and almost without any help. It was manager training, the toughest thing imaginable. Eight of them had started the venture, the third in the last five years. A year ago, they had gone through

hell - each on their own. One of them was caught out, went missing and never turned up again. Another was rescued after a two-day search at the end of his tether.
His equipment consisted only of a Swiss army knife, a small rucksack, a three metre long rope and the clothes he was wearing. It wasn't much and it could get uncomfortably chilly there at night. He remembers freezing more at night than he was at that moment. No, the ferry accident is nothing more than a practice session in the city forest compared to the last survival training.

The first helicopters with searchlights appear in the sky. The burgeoning certainty of foreseeable survival takes complete possession of him. No painful memory disturbs David at this moment. His imagination has long since overcome the vague cold attack on his body. He once again imagines the cold nights in the jungle, the worms and crawling insects on which he had fed. This ferry disaster is a walk in the park for him compared to the demands on his tested survival skills. David is a tough man who leaves nothing to chance.

He sees illuminated boats appear on the horizon. Half an hour later, he can make out five lifeboats with broad beams of light directed at the water.

This massively sluggish rescue infrastructure makes David impatient after all; it still takes three and a half hours before the circling light of the boat "Mona" locates him. They had spent too long searching for large pieces of wreckage, probably even counting on at least one rubber dinghy, from which between 50 and 100 survivors could have been rescued in one go. David is a meagre yield for the enormous rescue machinery.

The "Mona" manoeuvres up to David on the port side. Two rescuers are lowered to him via a beam and a pulley. David is looking forward to the sympathy he will receive. He no longer thinks about those who died in the disaster. In his euphoric mind's eye, the headline in the Irish Times the next day shines:

"The attempt to rescue the sole survivor from the Irish Sea after the sinking of the "Irish Future" ended in tragedy...".

***

Haiku

Capturing life,
suppressing certain death,
vanity is realised.
***

Vanity loses
infinite power in being
before it dries up.
***

Traces in the snowy land,
life carried far and wide,
blowing away in the wind.
***

Your life determines
its melody of fate
and allows you to grow.
***

Time dilation,
ego trapped in space
in the web of consciousness.
***

In the spring morning,
a symphony
composes the day.

The Rat King of Dublin

As you all probably know, I'm an excellent conversationalist when it comes to animals. Well, maybe the newcomers among you don't know it yet, those can simply take the following story as a fable. However, I will reveal to the initiated that this story was told to me first hand by a sewer rat, which was completely insignificant in this story, but was able to observe everything from the background. It is so inconspicuous that neither friend nor foe noticed it. I would say it was the smartest rat in the sewers of Dublin. So today I can tell you the story of a megalomaniac rat." Then George O'Flaherty begins:

* * *

Deep down in the sewers of Dublin once lived a great ruler, the Rat King Brandon. With cunning and strength he had managed to control the area near the Ports, up the Liffey to the Guinness Brewery. Across the Liffey, he controlled the canalisation along the length of O 'Connell Street to the General Post Office (GPO). It was here that the enemy formations of the Rat Lord Winston had put up considerable resistance to Brandon's attempt to take control of the sewers. Brandon's troops were beaten back, leaving

Winston in control of the area beyond the GPO. This defeat angered Brandon and he began to devise a cunning and devious war plan against Winston.

 In order to win a new battle, he had to have allies. Brandon did not like allies, but necessity now outweighed any reservations. The most cunning option seemed to him to be to join forces with a common enemy. By this, however, Brandon did not simply mean fraternising with any other rat lord, no, the alliance had to be with a categorical enemy of the rats. Only the unbelievable betrayal of their own kind would guarantee the prospect of the complete destruction of the rats behind Winston. But who came into question? Only humans or cats, really.

It was impossible to communicate with humans, they always struck out immediately. At the slightest approach, they panicked and hit rats with everything they had at their disposal. No, humans were simply too stupid, and so Brandon rejected the idea of allying himself with them. That left the cats. He shuddered at the thought of having to make common cause with the cats. How many times had they been a terrible nuisance to him, ravaged his soldiers and eaten some of his best officers. But the most horrible memory he had was of a fight to the death with a mighty cat, Captain Kevin of Grafton Street. He was a great cat leader and ruled the entire centre. He was allied with almost all the cat lords of Dublin. You could say he was the most powerful cat in Dublin, and Brandon had once come face to face with him. The fight was terrible and the thought of it caused a nasty stabbing pain in his left flank. Kevin had cut a deep wound here and bitten out a piece of flesh the size of a hen's egg. But Brandon had fought bravely and in turn inflicted a large scar on the captain, which has since disfigured Kevin's face from his eye to his nose. It would almost have been Brandon's last fight if it hadn't been for Sèan, his loyal adjutant. He had bravely thrown himself into the fight and distracted Kevin from him. But Sèan was no match for the mighty cat and had to pay for his loyalty with his life. The memory of these terrible events made Brandon think again about a possible co-operation with the humans. But how should he come to terms with them? The cats had found a way of communicating with the humans, and in most cases they were treated well by them. In some cases, humans even treated cats with affection. Brandon became a little jealous, as he had already tried to form a cat-like bond with humans. This one and only attempt almost turned into a disaster. It was in the old library on the Liffey. The door to the street was open because some people were carrying something into the building. Brandon had taken this opportunity to slip into the old house. Shoo, up a few steps and he suddenly found himself in a large room. There were books everywhere, on the walls and on the tables. Directly opposite the entrance, roughly in the centre of the room, stood a huge desk, behind which sat a scrawny man with white hair. Brandon stood reverently in front of the desk, just as he had once seen a small cat do in a similar situation.

Brandon was sitting under a cupboard at the time, looking at a kitchen table where a fat woman was sitting and cutting meat. The cat trotted through the door and crouched right in front of the kitchen table. The woman saw them, rose from her chair and spoke words that Brandon didn't understand, but which sounded friendly and tender. The cat meowed flattering songs that made Brandon feel sick in his hiding place. But the friendly woman picked the wooing animal up from the ground, caressed it and held a piece of sliced meat in front of its dripping mouth. A wet meow, then the seductress snatched the longed-for piece and devoured it. Her next meow was not long in coming; Brandon could not ignore the begging undertone. The intended effect did not fail to materialise. She was kindly handed another piece of the desired treat. This was repeated many times under Brandon's envious eyes, but he saw no chance of getting any of it, the cat was in full control of the situation.

Brandon was now sitting in front of that old desk in the library, hoping for a similar reaction from the scrawny man - even though he didn't smell meat. But the man didn't seem to notice him, so Brandon tried to get his attention with sweet squeals. No sooner had he emitted his rat-cajoling than the man looked at him wide-eyed for a moment, jumped up with a violent leap and rushed to the nearby fireplace. He made noises that sounded nothing like those of the friendly woman. Brandon sensed that things were developing differently here than between humans and cats, but he didn't want to withdraw his offer of friendship to the humans prematurely. So he waited to see how things developed and kept making a tender rat sound. The man, however, grabbed a thick, dangerous-looking black pole with a pointed hook at the

bottom. With this he lunged at Brandon, and as
he approached him he drew the black monster of
hooks over his white head and uttered loud,
savage and hideous sounds. Brandon guessed
that this man was not going to hand him meat as
the hook came down on him, the next moment
he had the painful certainty. The hook grazed his
shoulder and tore a thumb-width strip out of his
fur. He now knew that rats could not negotiate
with humans.

 He rejected the idea of co-operating with the
humans. With the cats, he could understand the
hostility, as it was mutual. With them, he could
also recognise hostile intentions; they would
openly go into battle. But the humans? You
don't even notice their hostility and then they
suddenly strike. No, you can't form an alliance
with humans. Should he perhaps put the GPO's
sewerage system out of his mind? That was also
unthinkable. Winston had to be driven out,
because the GPO belonged under the king's
control.

Brandon therefore decided to meet with the cat
captain Kevin, but he didn't dare approach him
directly. So he decided to make a diplomatic
approach.

 There were usually a few cats hanging around

the O'Connell statue at night, but they were rather harmless. They were young tomcats courting two or three adolescent cats. Brandon decided to involve them in the diplomatic service. He called for his new adjutant, Cathel.

"I need a meeting with the cat captain Kevin of Grafton Street, I want to make a deal with him that should be of great benefit to him. Have one of the young tomcats from the O'Connell go to him, you have nothing to fear from them. I expect the answer tonight. Let Kevin decide the time and place of the meeting."

The adjutant hurried off immediately. "Aleae acta est" thought Brandon. There was no turning back now, and he had no choice but to refine his rough battle plan against Winston.
 It was already early in the morning when Cathel scratched at the drainpipe to his chamber. Brandon eagerly invited him to come in; Cathel crawled up obsequiously, grinning, aware of the favourable news he was permitted to deliver. He skilfully kept silent, increasing the king's impatience.
 "So what?" Brandon shouted.
 "Ahem," coughed the adjutant, "it's all settled."
 "What?" the king blurted out, biting the aide's throat.

"Appointment," gasped the aide.

"When? Where?" roared the rat king.

"Would you mind letting go," the aide pleaded. Brandon released his teeth from his aide's throat. Without further ado, Cathel began:

"Kevin would be pleased to receive your Excellency at the Molly Malone tomorrow around midnight. The Captain proposes that a maximum of five cats and five rats be allowed to accompany him. If Your Excellency agrees to this proposal, we need make no further arrangements and can arrive at the Molly Malone tomorrow. But if your Excellency..."

"Hold your tongue," the king ordered, "call four of the strongest soldiers to accompany us, you take command. But position five hundred soldiers on the far bank of the Liffey and post one every twenty metres as far as Grafton Street. The army shall be ready for action at the Molly Malone in less than three minutes, should it become necessary."

"Very well, Your Excellency, I will arrange everything," humphed the adjutant.

"The troops on the Liffey shall have taken up their position about twenty-three o'clock. We shall also set out from here at that time."

The adjutant lay down on his back in front of the king as a sign of his subservience until he ordered him away.

The next night, at the agreed hour, there was a scratching on the king's drainpipe.

"I'm ready," Brandon said and scurried out to the five waiting men. They scrambled silently down the path towards Grafton Street and were there about forty minutes before the appointed time. There was

no one here, if you didn't count the oddly staggering people who stumbled past Molly from time to time. But they didn't care about the rats, so there was obviously no danger from them. When the rats had scouted the immediate area, the rat king ordered: "There's

nothing suspicious, I think we can trust the cats. So let's wait and see."

The cats were on time, but only the captain could be seen. With his head raised proudly and his tail rising majestically into the air, he trotted towards Molly Malone from the direction of Stevens Green. Brandon felt a shiver run down his spine when he saw this proud cat. He looked even more powerful than he remembered. When he had almost reached Molly, his scar was also visible.

'It would be really good if he became our ally,' Brandon thought.

So as not to arouse suspicion, he tripped out

from under Molly and moved a few metres towards Kevin. He felt the stinging pain in his loins, but he tried not to think about it. The cat trotted towards him unimpressed. When he reached the rat, he stopped and sat down abruptly in front of it, wasting no time.
"You have a proposition?"
 "An offer," Brandon said, "you know the Winston?"
 "The one from the GPO? Of course, a tough bloke, and clever. He's played many a trick on me, the little sod."
Satisfied, Brandon replied:
"Then it won't be inconvenient for you if I deliver him to you, free of charge, so to speak."
 Kevin licked his mouth with relish.
 "Not at all, it will be my pleasure. But how are you going to do that?"
 "Slow down," Brandon said, "I have to make a small condition, not much, but it should be said."
The cat began to lick his fur leisurely, then stopped abruptly and whispered: "Well
, name your condition." Brandon now thought it appropriate to make an impression as well. So, turning to his adjutant, he said:
"Cathel, make our ideas known to the captain."
 The adjutant snapped out of the apathy into

which he had sunk since the encounter, unaware that he would be given the floor.
"Ahem," he began, somewhat embarrassed and a little confused, "well." He cleared his throat and spoke up:

"Well, what your majesty means, er, I mean, your majesty says there's a condition."
 The cat didn't even glance at the aide. Turning to Brandon, he hissed:

"You already said that, Brandon!" The king hissed at his aide:

"I already told him that, explain the condition to the captain."
 The adjutant had caught himself by now and began without further ado.
 "Your Majesty offers to lure Prince Winston and his soldiers into a trap in which it will no longer be a problem for you, Captain, to destroy him. In return, Your Majesty will ask the GPO for sovereignty over the canalisation. This would allow him to control the entire area north of O'Connell Street. As cats and rats have different needs in most cases, the whole thing could be organised in such a way that we don't get into each other's way. The points that affect common interests would have to be regulated by contract, but there aren't many. We are offering

to leave
 this regulation entirely to the cats in return. We see no obstacles to an agreement."
 The adjutant had finished his little speech and slumped down again. Brandon was satisfied, he couldn't have said it any better. He looked at Kevin expectantly. The cat began to lick his fur again with relish. He now performed the ritual much more thoroughly. The rat king became a little nervous, his fur bristled and the tip of his tail began to tremble.
 "Well, Captain," he interrupted the silence. But Kevin was not distracted from his washing. He had now worked his fur down to his tail. Brandon paced back and forth excitedly until the captain suddenly said, "
Tell me your plan."
The rat king stopped tensely and asked,
"Does that mean they agree?"
 "We'll see," said the cat and began to lick his paws. Brandon decided that now was no longer the time for showmanship and began to explain the plan in person and without further ado:
"I challenge Winston to a final battle, a battle that will grant
 the winner dominion over the sewers in the entire central area of Dublin. I will choose an area for the battle where Winston feels he has

superiority, he cannot let such an offer go to waste. It's well within the area he controls, in Wolfe Tone Street. He will feel safe there. We will move openly from O'Connell Street into Mary Street during the night, Winston and his henchmen will let us come undisturbed, but will have all their men busy watching us. It will be easy for him to close our return route starting from the GPO, so that we will be trapped afterwards. Winston will certainly not miss this opportunity. Here comes the opportunity for you cats. Winston won't have the entrance from the Liffey via Channel Street watched because he sees us moving in openly from O'Connell Street. He won't dream of our alliance, so he'll feel unbeatable. If Winston's spies see us move from the Liffey to O'Connell Street, the Prince will withdraw all observers in the other catchment areas. You can then get to Wolfe Tone Street unseen and be there before us. You can hide there and wait until I move in with my army. Winston will have the other direction blocked off from Wolfe Tone Street, leaving us no way out. You can have some of your soldiers remove this barricade unit so that this street will no longer allow Winston's people to escape. We will have an easy game. An hour later, Winston and his rats will no longer exist. You and I will

be the absolute rulers of Dublin's centre, you in the upper world, me in the lower world."
 The Rat King had now finalised his plan and stared at Kevin expectantly. He had not stopped licking his paws and gave no indication that he intended to do so any time soon. He didn't even look up after Brandon had finished. After an impatient while, Brandon said,
"So what?"
Kevin suddenly stopped his licking ritual and whispered:
"We'll see, I'll let you know."
 The cat suddenly got up and trotted up Grafton Street. Brandon looked at his aide in amazement:
"That arrogant cat," he shouted, "what's the show? He can't want to say no on this occasion."
 "He didn't either."
 "That's true, but why is he hesitating? There's nothing more to think about."
 "Diplomatic tactics," surmised the adjutant, "you know how cats are."
 The cats kept the rat king in suspense for three days. Towards the evening of the third day, a messenger from the captain reached Brandon and informed him that his master was in agreement and asked the king to arrange the combat meeting with the prince of the GPO. He

would then need the exact schedule at least three days before that date.

They could now consider themselves allies.

Brandon's rat heart leapt for joy when he saw the pact with the cats finalised. Perhaps as early as next week, he would be the undisputed ruler of the entire sewerage system in Dublin city centre. The area of Mary Street behind the GPO in particular was a land of milk and honey for rats, as market stalls were set up here every day, from which the biggest delicacies fell. There was no longer any need to go to the trouble of obtaining food at the risk of their lives by entering residential buildings. There at the market, rats could eat almost unmolested. The thought of this put Brandon in a somnambulistic state. After wallowing in these expectations for a long time, he called Cathel, his adjutant, to him and he arrived immediately. He immediately noticed the boss's good mood and therefore took the liberty of skipping the usual submissive ritual, especially as the king began without further ado:

"Look at me, adjutant. Before you stands the future autocrat of Dublin City."

Cathel thought it appropriate to make a slight gesture of loyalty after all. The king accepted it graciously and said:

"You, my loyal adjutant, will betray me."
 "But your majesty," Cathel said indignantly.
 "Let me finish, my friend. Of course you will betray me with my consent. I haven't told you the whole plan yet, I had to make sure of your loyalty first. So listen:
"You will go over to Winston tonight with my deputy troop commander. You will tell him that you have taken leave from me on important business so that I will not suspect anything. Justify your betrayal with my insane plan to launch a futile attack against the ruler of the GPO. We plan to invade the enemy territory on the night of the third day, starting today, in order to occupy it. Tell him our route of entry and the time. We will send out scouts over the next few days to show them the seriousness of our plan. If they have any doubts about your defection, they should be dispelled. You will work to get Winston to concentrate all his troops on our route and later withdraw them to Wolfe Tone Street. Give them strategic clues that appear to be to their advantage but are actually beneficial to us. Don't mention the cats under any circumstances. They mustn't find out about our trump card. Nobody knows our plan except the two of us, the commander and the deputy commander. This ensures that nothing can leak

out. You are bound by this order until the cats appear. Then you will spectacularly defect back to us." Cathel was genuinely impressed by his king's cunning.

"Magnificent," he said, "simply brilliant. This will surely make us the sole rulers of the realm." "One more thing: if you do

a good job, I'll appoint you governors, you'll get West Liffey and the deputy will get East Liffey. So you see, it pays for you to be cunning. You are therefore officially given the assignment for this mission. The deputy has already been informed. In the meantime, keep quiet about the upcoming promotion, as this could make the commander disgruntled, as he considers such a promotion more appropriate for himself than for his deputy. The commander is a good soldier, but I believe that you will be the better governor. I don't want any conflict before the battle. Afterwards, he will simply have to accept my decision."

"Not a word," the flattered adjutant assured him, "Your Majesty will be completely satisfied with me as always."

"I should think so," said the king, "you are now dismissed for your mission."

Cathel took his leave with double honour.

"One more thing," the king called after the

adjutant, "inform the cat captain of our schedule so that he can be there on time."
"No problem, that will be done immediately," said the future governor and disappeared.
 The days flew by, and that was a good thing. Brandon could hardly wait for the day of the battle. As planned, he had sent scouts into enemy territory and they had remained unmolested. Cathel and the deputy did a great job. During this time, a tense silence prevailed, and if an enemy rat was encountered, it was politely reserved, almost friendly. On the other hand, the battle was also eagerly awaited. Brandon's plan worked perfectly.

The day had finally arrived. The Rat King had received word from Kevin that the cats would be there on time, nothing was left to chance. Towards evening, just as the evening star was rising, the Rat King's troops gathered on the north bank of the Liffey in front of O'Connell Street. It was a formidable march. Brandon was proud when he saw his army, moved by the idea that at the end of the night he would be the absolute ruler of this city. Nothing could stand in the way of his glorious victory, and in this consciousness he tripped with his head held high in front of his soldiers. The few people who were still passing by at the time were disgusted when they saw the rats marching up. It must have been about an hour after midnight when the king's commander gave the order to start. The King kept behind him and his officers and the march through O'Connell Street got under way. At a leisurely pace they pushed on to the GPO, turned into enemy territory on Mary Street and trotted almost like a travelling party towards Wolfe Tone Street. As expected, they remained unmolested. The group of officers finally reached O'Connell Street. They felt a little queasy. So they paused for a moment before giving the order to march in. It all happened very quickly now. As soon as Brandon's troops had fully marched into Wolfe Tone Street, enemy rats from Winston's troops came from almost every nook and cranny. Within minutes, Brandon's rats were surrounded. A terrible slaughter began, thousands of Brandon's soldiers were bitten to death by the enemy rats. Brandon wondered where the cats were, it had all been arranged. But then he saw his adjutant. Cathel was firing at the enemy troops and Brandon struggled to get through to him.

"What are you doing? " Brandon is very angry.
 "I'm carrying out your orders," said Cathel, "I'm

going to lie behind you until the cats come."
"But they're not coming," cried the king.
 "Orders are orders," replied the adjutant.
"But I now order you to fight on our side."
 "I can't obey that, the first order was to serve
Winston until the cats strike. But the cats haven't
struck yet, so I have to wait."
 "But the order was mine, I can cancel it."
 "Not at this moment, I am bound by the first
order of my king, which cannot be cancelled by
anything in the world."
 Brandon could only just realise how devastating
blind obedience could be, but this realisation
came too late. He didn't have the chance to think
about it any more. His arch-enemy Winston
jumped on his back at that moment and sank his
teeth into his neck. He fought back with all his
might and managed to shake off the rat lord.
Bleeding, he ran back in the direction of Mary
Street. He saw his army being routed. He had to
get away. This battle was unwinnable, for the
enemy were outnumbered. At that moment,
hundreds of cats suddenly leapt out of the
surrounding houses. Brandon paused, a new
hope flickering inside him. The cats had only
been delayed and the tide could still turn.
Together with them, they would still be
victorious despite the wounds they had suffered.

Feeling like a glorious ruler again, he trotted back into the carnage of the fighting rats. He found his adjutant and called out to him:
"The cats are here."
The aide said, "
Your Majesty can count on me," as the swipe of a cat's paw cut him down. Brandon watched in horror as the cats pounced on all the rats, regardless of which group they belonged to. He saw his deputy commander being mauled to death by an overpowering cat. The next moment, hundreds of people rushed out of the houses on Wolfe Tone Street. They were holding boards in their hands, each with a long pointed nail sticking out of the end, and they were beating all the rats. Brandon recognised the cruel play of these terrible weapons.
 'We rats must unite,' Brandon thought. This realisation came too late. He was struck in the loin by a sharp blow, the iron spike penetrating deep into his body. Brandon realised
that an evil-looking man, it was the librarian from the Liffey, was lifting the board with a mighty swing, and he was torn into the air by the nail. Then it went dark around him.

When Brandon woke up, dawn was already breaking. The first thing he noticed were people, men who all seemed to look the same. They carried brooms and shovels; a large car drove alongside them. Brandon saw these men taking his dead army and the former enemy soldiers of Prince Winston on shovels and throwing them into the large car. He could see all this through the gap of two boards of a crate he had somehow ended up in. Brandon had to get away before the humans discovered him. With difficulty, his whole body aching, he crawled over the edge of the crate, which fortunately wasn't too high, and ran along the wall of a house until he reached a door that was ajar. He scurried inside, no-one seemed to be here. He immediately recognised the cupboard, which was so far away from the wall that he could crawl behind and under it.

It was dark, he couldn't recognise anything, but he could feel and smell it. As fate would have it, Winston was the only one, apart from him, to have survived this carnage and fled to the same hiding place. The two of them went at each other like two hunted roosters. The prince sank his sharp teeth into the king's shoulder. Tearing himself a deep, bleeding wound, he managed to free himself. With his mouth wide open, Brandon quickly grabbed his enemy's throat and bit down with all his might. He felt the warm blood of his hated opponent flowing down his throat and only let go when Winston stopped moving.

 Brandon sank to his side, mortally wounded. His whole body ached as if he was being mauled by ten cats.

He had finally done it, he was the absolute ruler of the city's sewerage system. Despite the cats' deceit, he was now the undisputed rat king of Dublin for a moment.

Transience of power (Poetry)

So sweet the power, covet'd as whole fruit,
Fulfils the dream that took away his love;
Though nearly dying of desire mute,
succumbs the ruler to by his own rove.

His greed within, knows neither friend nor foe,
steals him the breath within a wrong delight,
it suffocates the longing burning glow,
the love now dies he's sick and without light.

Deception pulls him into games of might,
to which alone he brings the toll of love.
goes into battle with faux Friends to fight
before the fool drawn into evil rove.

Succumbs in death still vanity appears,
falls into nil, he has no time for fears.

The secret of life (poetry)

Life is a sphere
on whose surface we live.
We have every freedom to move around
on this surface.
Sometimes we cross points that
we have already touched,
déjà vu.
But we know nothing of the depth of this sphere,
it lies beyond our imagination.
We do not realise
that the centre is not in our lives,
but in this depth.

Little Busybody and Chameleony

What's the difference between dreams and illusions,"

George introduces his last story. It seems to be his favourite topic.

"Many people find it difficult to distinguish between them. Both are ideas of a world as it could be, but is not yet. However, while dreams can be realised and are very often goal-oriented, illusions never lead to the goal. Both can occasionally trigger feelings of happiness when you imagine a desirable future state. The dreamer can realise his dream, but the illusionist never does. As the saying goes, he rides a dead horse and hopes that it will take him to his goal.

In my current story, there is a very mean villain who talks people out of their dreams and showers them with illusions. Let the listener decide for themselves whether this only exists in fairy tales."

* * *

Once upon a time there was a little busybody who believed that all people were evil. As he believed himself to be good, he suffered greatly under these circumstances, especially as he was small and weak and could do nothing against all these evil people on his own. So, she decided to flee from the world and the evil people. He got a magic potion from a witch, which made him invisible to people in his own form and put him into a deep sleep with beautiful dreams. When the little man took this potion for the first time, he dreamt that he had grown up to be a big, strong man who could now venture out among the humans.

In reality, however, Little Busybody was not sleeping, but had turned into the large, malicious and selfish Chameleony.

Chameleony is a human-like creature that can take on a seemingly loving and good-natured or evil and scheming character, depending on what it likes and what is convenient.

The dream led the little man to believe that he was good and could take away evil from people in human form. In reality, however, Chameleony went to them to spread hatred and discord and to steal their dreams. Using cunning and trickery, he managed to steal the dreams of most of them, as they were the price the witch demanded for the potion.

When the effects of the potion wore off, Chameleony felt Little Busybody's weaknesses returning.

So, he retired with the captured dreams.

Chameleony turned back into Little Busybody.

Although the dream he had experienced was very beautiful, he realised that something was wrong and he felt bad and miserable. But then the witch appeared and promised that he would soon feel better if he would only give her all dreams, he had brought with him. The little male left them to her without suspicion, as they were of no value to him, as he had no memory of the chameleonity.

He soon received another drink from her, gulped it down greedily and fell back into a deep sleep. This time too, the little man dreamt a beautiful dream, but it was nowhere near as beautiful as the first time. He saw himself transformed into a handsome man again, going to the people and telling them how evil they were. He told them to take an example from him, who had only good intentions and wanted to free them, the people, from wickedness and depravity. But the people laughed at him and told him to go to hell and try his luck there.

In reality, of course, Little Busybody wasn't asleep again, but had turned into this mischievous chameleony, only he was a little more scheming and devious than the first time.

When he went into town, the first people he met were the people of the Lowlands, whom he had not yet harmed. He had been very charming and kind to them, despite his malice, because he was a chameleony.

These people still liked him because of this and so it was no wonder that they trusted him blindly.

But there were also the others in the Highlands that he had visited before he went to the Lowlanders. He had talked them out of their dreams with cunning and deceitful promises. But as these were not enough for him, he had also persuaded them to borrow more dreams from his current friends, the Lowlanders. He only needed them for a short time, he told them, and he would personally return them to the Lowlanders the next day. However, he had claimed to the Lowlanders that the Highlanders would pay the debt themselves and he left them in this belief. Some time had passed since then and he had brought no dreams with him. The people of the Highlands feared they would never see their dreams again, but hoped that he had at least settled the debt with the Lowlanders. As they would also have liked to have their own dreams back, the Highlanders set off in the direction of the Lowlands.

The Highlands and Lowlands are separated by a lake that was only travelled by a ferry. For this reason, the inhabitants generally exchanged information by shouting, which was transported and altered by a special echo. When the Lowlanders heard that the Highlanders had gathered on the far shore of the lake, they also made their way to the shore on this side. To reach it, they had to descend a dangerous slope at the end. They therefore gratefully accepted Chameleony's offer; he had agreed to make the descent for them in order to be their mouthpiece.

Now it was the case that only an echo-distorted version of the call could be received above. Chameleony was well aware of this and, cunning as he was, he was able to use it to his advantage. Once down on the lake shore, he called out to the Highlanders:

"Do you have the dreams of my friends?"

He shouted it just loud enough for the Lowlanders above to understand the question. But a sentence inverted by the strange echo reached the other bank:

"My friends have the dreams." That's why they call back:

"Have you got ours too? Let the ferryman bring them to us." The Lowlanders up on the hillside shoulder only understood "ferryman" and "bring". They asked Chameleony and he replied:

"They said the ferryman would bring them to you."

The ferryman Aideen McCoilté was a true Irishman and God-fearing. He lived in the Midlands and cared little for the affairs of Highlanders and Lowlanders. Besides, it was Friday and Fridays were the ferryman's day off:

"If God called this day Friday, he knows why," Aideen used to say, because he had worked in Germany for two years and liked to adopt the German meaning of the days of the week.

Chameleony knew, of course, that Aideen didn't sail on Fridays, and so his scheme went undetected for that day. It was agreed that Tuesday would be the day to hire the ferryman, as Tuesday in German meaning is nothing else than workday, and that's why it was the only day that Aideen moved his ferry. Aideen had watertight reasons: Saturday and Sunday are weekends, and only crazy people work then, and Aideen McCoilté was by no means crazy. Aideen went blue on Monday, because for an Irishman, blue Monday is something of a bank holiday, or so he argued. The German name for Wednesday is 'midweek', that's why Wednesdays are to be honoured like the weekends. There is no reasonable reason to believe that the middle of the week should not be celebrated in the same way as the weekend, otherwise would they have bothered to name it as a day of the week? In fact, Aideen celebrated Wednesday particularly extensively. As Wednesday was more or less a Sunday, Thursday was something like a Monday.

Working on Thursdays was comparable to desecrating Blue Monday. Besides, Thursday is the day of thunder and everyone knows how dangerous it is to work on the water during thunderstorms.

Behind closed doors - they didn't want to mess things up with him - many people said that Aiden was just lazy. It can't be dismissed out of hand, but that's for others to decide.

On Tuesday, however, Aideen McCoilté worked like a man possessed every time.

"If God called this day Workday, he must have had his reason. But if he had wanted us to work on other days as well, all these days would have been called Tuesday (German: Workday).

But since there was only one, we only had to work on that day. It was a model that Aideen could live with.

So, there was no way of persuading the ferryman to transport the dreams before Tuesday. Chameleony knew all this, of course, and he was able to spin his web of intrigue on it. He would think of something by Tuesday and so he let the High and Lowlanders believe that the ferryman would bring them their dreams on Tuesday. Everyone was happy and eagerly awaited Tuesday.

Chameleony noticed how the potion wore off and Little Busybody's weakness took possession of him.

When Little Busybody woke up, he felt very miserable.

The dreams of his good deeds did not satisfy him. Chameleony 's experiences came into his mind in a shadowy way, without him realising what was going on, but he felt that it was not good. The little male was unable to categorise the dreams he had experienced and the memories of his experiences as a chameleony that were forcing themselves upon him and fell into a deep depression. The good from his dreams and Chameleony began to fight within him, but the little male was too weak to cope with this inner struggle. He sensed that he would never be allowed to drink this magic potion again, but knew that he would be too weak to refuse it. So, it decided to die. Once it had made this decision, it immediately felt better. The depression receded and at that moment the witch appeared.

Little Busybody refused the offered potion because he had decided to die.

"Ha," said the witch, "that's just right; because if you've decided to die anyway, you can't lose anything.

I'll make your drink a little stronger so that you'll have some extra nice dreams. The only reward I ask for is your spent dreams when you wake up again."

The witch's arguments convinced the little male, and he also felt an insatiable craving for this drink. The witch brewed a concoction that was many times stronger than the previous one. This time she wanted to make an impact as soon as Chameleony woke up.

When the little male had emptied the offered cup to the brim, he fell into a deeper sleep than he had ever experienced before.

In the dream, it woke up as a man, strong and self-confident. This time he was sure that he could change people. With this awareness, he went out into the world to complete his work.

In fact, Chameleony woke up more evil, scheming and devious than he had ever been. In this state, the witch intercepted him.

"I have to talk to you because your other self is about to commit a folly. I've made the potion strong enough this time so that you don't have to turn back into that pathetic Little Busybody, because that would be your certain death. It's Tuesday tomorrow and you have your appointment. Go and bring me all their dreams, you can't leave any of them behind. That's the price of your new life. But I won't let you go empty-handed. I'll give you a hundred horses loaded with illusions. Bring them to the people, tell them they are their dreams with compound interest. People won't realise the difference, if at all, then much later. It will be easy for you to get hold of the rest of their dreams, as they expect to make plenty of profit in a short space of time. Illusions are worthless to me, so you can be generous with them.

Use them only for our purpose."

Thus, equipped with illusions, Chameleony set

off in the direction of the Lowlands. He left fifty loaded horses outside the village and entered the town with the others. When he met the inhabitants, he offered them the illusions stored on these fifty horses:

"These dreams are sent to you by the Highlanders in return for what you have borrowed; anything beyond that is your gain. They let it be known that they will always be happy to do business with you."

The number of illusions, which they mistook for dreams, was so abundant that it left them speechless.

With the remaining fifty loaded horses outside the village, Chameleony travelled to the shore of the lake that separated the Highlands from the Lowlands.

The ferryman was already waiting there, as it was Tuesday. They loaded the horses onto the ferry and began the journey towards the Highlands.

During the three-hour journey, Chameleony also tried his luck with Aideen McCoillté and offered him ten illusions for one of his dreams. Of course, he didn't tell him that they were illusions.

But Aideen waved it off with a smile.

"If God had wanted me to have more dreams than the ones he has given me, he would have given them to me. So, what am I supposed to do with dreams that I can't use? Slán a'bhaile (Irish: Come home safely)", said Aideen, and that was the end of the matter for him.

But the Highlanders were blinded by the supposed wealth. They greedily absorbed all the illusions. In the euphoria caused by these illusions, Chameleony proposed his devious business to the Highlanders. He would need all the dreams they could muster. The Highlanders pointed out that all their dreams were less than what he had brought them. As Chameleony was not interested in taking back the illusions he had brought, he said:

"I'll be careful not to take your newly acquired winnings from you again. Your friends, the Lowlanders, will be happy to help you give me what I need. But they too shall keep the dreams I brought them in your name."

The Highlanders sent a negotiator by ferry to the Lowlanders. Seven hours later, the ferry arrived back in the Highlands with the negotiator. He had brought all the Lowlanders' dreams with him. It was easy, because people liked to trade their dreams for illusions.

In the end, Chameleony left High and Lowlands with twenty horses, loaded with the dreams of men. But the witch was never to receive these dreams.

Little Busybody's dream was so strong this time that the protagonist of the dream realised himself. He knew ad hoc that he was the other side of Chameleony. He realised that it was not good and evil that separated people, but the error of dream and illusion. He therefore decided to fight Chameleony of his ego and give people back their dreams. He went into battle against Chameleony.

* * *

Lonely and abandoned, a lifeless Little Busybody lies in the forest in front of the entrance to the world. His dream had defeated Chameleony! The protagonist of the powerful dream had wrested the captured dreams from him and brought them back to the people. However, they were no longer willing to part with the illusions. So it is that even today, every dream is followed by five illusions.

But Little Busybody died from an overdose of the magic potion.

Aphrodite (Lyrical Prose)

I have left the safe shore.
Leaderless, the dreamboat drifts towards an
uncertain future.
Flooded by the magic of a new beginning, I don't
dare to steer.
My present melts into a veil of mist,
dissolves into the foam of abandoned time.
When the one born in foam rises to Olympus,
her charm has filled the ether.
Her radiance melts the shore left behind into
nothingness.
I place myself trustingly in the hands of the
creative friend of man,
receive from him the purifying fire
and the new-born strength to ascend to Olympus.

The Dublin Ophthalmologist Ripper

We were once again sitting round the fireplace in Joyce's Bar when a man came in wearing a kind of cowboy hat that I hadn't seen here before. But the others seemed to know him. One of my friends whispered to me:

"This is Jeremias from Dublin and he comes to Kiltimagh every now and then to visit his grandparents who live up in the mountains. He always brings a hair-raising but funny story with him. Let's see what he has in store today."

After Jeremias had got himself a pint of beer, he sat down. One of them asked what was new.

"You won't believe me," Jeremias began, "but I've received a tip-off about a ripper from Dublin who has been up to mischief there for a long time. But it's best if I start from the beginning.

A few days ago, in the old library on the Liffey, I came across a forgotten booklet that, despite its obvious age, had never been read by anyone. When I opened the yellowed cover, I realised why. The strange title was handwritten on the starched paper:

Musicians and monsters

I bought the booklet for 20 pence and started reading it on the train to Claire Morris. I soon realised that I must have come into possession of the only original copy of a book about the story of Brandon the Ripper."

Then Jeremias, who had read the whole book on the train journey, told us.

The musician and the monster

Shortly after the turn of the twentieth century, a strange series of murders took place, which have gone down in history as the murders of the Dublin ophthalmologist-ripper.

The strange thing about these cases was that only ophthalmologists became victims of the mysterious Ripper. The murders invariably occurred on the nights of the seventeenth of March before St Patrick's Day. In the morning, a slashed and decapitated corpse with a blood-soaked white coat would usually be floating in the River Liffey, although police patrols had been stepped up since the Ripper's activities became known on the night in question. The murders stopped one day, just as they had begun. The Ripper was never caught.

Long before the first murder, the lazy and poor farmer Seán McLought lived in a cottage near Enfield in County Meath. Now laziness was no bad thing in this part of Ireland in those days and McLought, who rarely took on the disfiguring burden of labour, was a handsome man of good repute. His wife Laura was the most beautiful woman in the village and many a lad craned his neck for her when she went to mass in the morning.

The McLoughts had a daughter with a voice whose sound far outshone the songs of the nightingale. Everyone in the village knew this voice, but no one had ever seen this daughter, although the enchanted lads of the village never missed an opportunity to catch a glimpse of the voice's owner. Anyone with a voice like that must be incredibly beautiful.

It was no wonder the McLoughts never showed their daughter, because that poor brat was the spawn of ugliness. It's hard to describe how ugly Joeann was. Her face resembled a giant gecko face with advanced acne after an accident with a steamroller. At nine years old, she was already 1.90 metres tall and had the physique of a pregnant female orangutan after a crash with a herd of elephants. Her characteristic features manifested themselves with increasing age. However, growth was limited to the trunk, while the legs had already stopped growing by the age of seven. This somewhat unconventional construction of nature gave her a peculiar gait, which I probably don't need to describe to anyone. The girl's ugliness was so abysmal that her father could never bring himself to look at her in horror. As she was the McLoughts' only daughter, her father loved her dearly and with a guilty conscience, despite her pitiful appearance. The father suspected that the reason for his daughter's hideousness was his excessive consumption of poitín. Poitín is a home-made, eighty per cent barley spirit that tastes terrible and has a reputation for making people blind and impotent. The only attraction of this concoction was its illegality, as the production and possession of this spirit was strictly forbidden. Nevertheless, hardly any Irish home was without this potent poison, as its consumption was seen as a kind of rebellion against the English occupiers and is still celebrated illegally today in remembrance of independence. In short, Seán McLought believed in the patriotic crippling of his sperm and his idolatrous love for his ugly daughter was no less patriotic, he just couldn't bring himself to look at it.

What he didn't know was that Joeann was the result of his beautiful wife Laura's one and only fling with the Russian wrestling villain Ivan Bornikow, who once made a guest appearance in Dublin and was known as "Ivan the Terrible" on the catcher scene. Laura was very attracted to the animality of this monster at the time.

Unfortunately, almost all of Ivan Bornikows unfavourable dispositions had been passed on to Joeann. The only positive aspect of this Mendelian vicious circle was the voice of Ivan's great-grand-aunt, who was once called the Nightingale of St Petersburg.

So Seán McLoughts sperm were not the cause of Joeann's ugliness and they were not simply crippled, but had probably died the patriotic hero's death in the Poitín long ago, leaving him childless himself.

Firmly believing in the monstrous wisdom that there is a lid for every pot, he called his supposed daughter to him one day.

"You, my beloved daughter," he said disgustedly, his face turned away, "you shall go to Dublin to the school of the blind music master Brandon Walsh, who will train your talent as a singer and make you a great artist."

With tears in her eyes, the sensitive Joeann left her mother and so-called father a little later in an ox cart. While the groaning ox was still labouring out of the village with the heavy girl, the loving pseudo-father was gripped by a sense of relief that he had not experienced since his wedding. Seán would never see his cuckoo daughter again.

It should only be mentioned in passing that the sperm did not die a patriotic hero's death in illegal booze, as initially suspected, but rather lapsed into a kind of death-like lethargy at the sight of his monstrous daughter, which only dissipated after the loss of his beloved monster. It is known that his sperm recovered permanently from then on and that he later became the father of twelve beautiful children.

Joeann McLought arrived safe and sound at the blind music master in Dublin. While the completely exhausted ox was being taken to the emergency slaughter, she grabbed her meagre bundle and handed Brandon Walsh her little finger, which he mistook for her hand because of its size. Her first words with the sweetness of her voice enchanted the music master so much that he fell in love with Joeann ad hoc. She realised this very well and decided to behave sensitively and take her chance. In the time that followed, they grew closer very quickly. While Joeann surrendered herself completely musically and her almost perfect voice sounded even sweeter after a short time, she held herself back physically. Brandon Walsh had completely fallen for her, her voice was so charming. For physicality, however, she only offered him her mighty arm, which he took for her body and which he grew to love. During intercourse, she had developed a technique with her fingers that he would never have realised had he not orchestrated the catastrophe that followed:

The lover, enchanted by the sweetest voice his perfect hearing had ever heard, had only one fervent wish: to see his now-married Joeann. That's why he went to see Marc Feerick, a well-known ophthalmologist in Dublin at the time, who had a reputation for being able to cure rare eye diseases such as that of the music master. What the musician did not know. His blindness was traumatic and had been caused by an early experience in his childhood. But the ophthalmologist was an enchanted psychiatrist and recognised the cause of the ailment straight away. It only took a few well-paid sessions and

Brandon left the practice cured.

In the confusion of the events that suddenly flooded visually upon him, a single desire to look his beloved Joeann in the face crystallised visibly. He could hardly wait to get home. He hurried to Raglan Road, where he lived. Heart pounding, he hurried up the stairs to his parlour and threw open the door to the lounge where Joeann usually sat knitting.

A huge monster crouched on his couch, grinning.

"It's eaten her," it pounded in his head. He had only one thought left: to destroy the murderer of his beloved wife. Out of his mind, he rushed into the knight's hall of his flat and tore the sword out of the first suit of armour. With it, he rushed into the lounge to behead the monster.

Joeann knew nothing of his secret visits to the so-called eye doctor - after all, Brandon wanted to surprise her. When the armed, fiercely determined husband pounced on the supposed monster with his sword raised, she thought it was one of the wild sex variations that the music master occasionally indulged in. As usual, she gave him her arm so that he could let off steam. He groaned against it and as he gripped the arm to keep from falling to the ground, the feeling of the embrace seemed strangely familiar. A terrible suspicion flashed through him.

What happened next can be explained in a few words:

Driven by the terrible realisation, the music master stormed out of the house with his sword under his coat. He ran straight to O'Connell Street to the haunted psychiatrist Marc Feerick, slashed him open lengthways and cut off his head without a second thought. That night, the night before St Patrick's Day, he threw his victim into the nearby River Liffey. From then on, for the next 15 years, he was overcome by an irresistible compulsion to rib an ophthalmologist on the eve of this holiday. He never realised his mistake, because he should have murdered psychiatrists.

Master General Brandon Walsh, the Ripper of the Ophthalmologists, was killed in the 1916 Easter Rising at the General Post Office in O'Connell Street. Thus, in retrospect, Seán McLought had an indirect part in a patriotic event by raising his cuckoo daughter.

Nothing has been revealed about the fate of the unfortunate Joeann."

Jeremiah ended his story with this. But he added something else:

"Music master errors are widespread throughout the world. That's why more ophthalmologists have always been murdered than psychiatrists. That may well be the reason why so many psychiatrists are still up to mischief today."

"Is the source trustworthy?" one of the listeners asked with a laugh. Everyone laughed, including Jeremiah.

"Absolutely," he said, "why would anyone doubt that?"

Haiku

The flower of bliss
the fair breath of glimpse lifetime
are found by the wise.
***

The best of being
is the sure expected death
before it hits us.
***

When a wise man dies,
he loses just one life
the world loses all.
***

The phoenix rises
and he fertilises the life
anew it every day.
***

To glide in a dream
and to be in happy love
is the highest bliss.
***

Constant happiness
will not make our dreams come true,
but perseverance.